"You can't leave until we've had our dance."

"I know, but here…?"

"Here. Right here. Right now." His voice had taken on a note of command, and then it softened. "Please," he said, and opened his arms.

He saw the little lift of her breasts and knew she'd caught her breath. Would she turn him down? If she did, he'd be a gentleman and let her go.

The hell with that. He hadn't made a fortune by being a gentleman. If she said no he'd pull her into his arms, bring her soft body against his, stroke his hands over her until she sighed and said yes to dancing with him, yes to making love with him, yes, yes, yes….

"Yes," Fallon whispered, and went into his arms.

Dear Reader,

The exciting, passion-filled story of the O'Connell family continues!

The Sicilian Surrender is the second book in my new family saga. Fallon O'Connell is a world-famous model. She doesn't enjoy living her life in the spotlight, but she's learned to accept it as part of her job. Stefano Lucchesi is the powerful CEO of a multinational corporation. He despises the paparazzi who stalk him and values his privacy above everything else. Fate brings these two people together in Sicily, an island simmering in the heat of the summer sun. But destiny has more planned for Fallon and Stefano than a simple chance encounter. A dark, rainy night. A narrow road. The squeal of tires, a car crash, and their lives are forever changed. Only love can heal Fallon, just as only love can reach Stefano's closely guarded heart.

As you discovered in my last family saga, THE BARONS, you can enjoy *The Sicilian Surrender* even if you haven't read the prior book, *Keir O'Connell's Mistress*. Join me on an exciting journey through the lives of a dynamic family. The O'Connells and I welcome you.

With love,

Sandra Marton

You can visit Sandra at
http://www.sandramarton.com or write to her at
P.O. Box 295, Storrs, Connecticut 06268, U.S.A.

Sandra Marton

THE SICILIAN SURRENDER

The O'CONNELLS

HARLEQUIN®

TORONTO • NEW YORK • LONDON
AMSTERDAM • PARIS • SYDNEY • HAMBURG
STOCKHOLM • ATHENS • TOKYO • MILAN • MADRID
PRAGUE • WARSAW • BUDAPEST • AUCKLAND

Special thanks to Joni Jones
for sharing her love of Sicily and its people with me.

ISBN 0-373-12350-7

THE SICILIAN SURRENDER

First North American Publication 2003.

Visit us at www.eHarlequin.com

Printed in U.S.A.

CHAPTER ONE

THE sun was a blurred golden orb in a lowering sky as the sirocco blew in from the sea, howling through the ruins of the *castello* like the voices of the rebellious gladiators who had once defended this bit of Sicily against the power and might of ancient Rome.

Stefano Lucchesi thought of those men as he mounted the last stone steps and stood on the top of the cliff. To the west, Mount Etna slumbered in the humid air. Below, the stormy waters of the Mediterranean pounded the rocky shore.

How many times had a sentry stood in this same place, watching for the enemy? Romans, Greeks, Arabs and Normans had all spilled their blood here in the name of dominion. Pirates had hunted offshore, lying in wait for unwary ships like packs of hungry wolves.

Invader after invader had conquered this land of his ancestors, until, at last, it shook free of its shackles and created enemies of its own, an aristocracy that grew fat on the sweat of those who tilled this rocky soil.

Stefano turned his back to the sea, dug his hands into the pockets of his jeans and surveyed his kingdom. Time had not treated it kindly. All that remained of the *castello* were tumbled stone walls and a handful of pillars.

Perhaps that was as it should be. There was a certain ironic justice in the way time had evened the balance sheet. What his great grandfather three times removed had built here, what his grandfather had ultimately lost in a feud so bitter it had ended in bloodshed, had long-ago crumbled to dust.

Even the land had been sold. Stefano had ordered his attorney to buy it back, piece by piece, from gnarled old men in baggy black suits who reminded him of his grandfather. Stefano had named a price that was more than fair, but the attorney's representatives had no success.

All the old men seemed eager to sell land that was basically dry and barren until they heard the buyer's name.

"Lucchesi?" they said.

One even spat on the ground by way of punctuation.

Stefano was amazed that the name should still evoke violent emotion after more than seventy years. He'd said so to his lawyer, who grinned, shook his head and said that Stefano needed to rent the *Godfather* movies and watch them from start to finish.

"It's the Mafia thing," Jack said. "How can you have Sicilian blood running through your veins and not understand? Those old guys knew your grandpa. They hated him. Why should you expect a welcome from them?"

Why, indeed?

Stefano knew little about the Mafia. He'd grown up in America, where his grandfather had immigrated decades before his birth. His father died when he was a baby and his mother, a New Orleans homecoming queen, dragged him from city to city in a frenzied search for excitement. Stefano was twelve when she died.

His paternal grandparents, who he hardly knew, took him in.

Tough, street smart, hiding his fear behind a mask of arrogance, he couldn't have been easy for them to handle. His grandmother fed him and clothed him and otherwise washed her hands of him. His grandfather tolerated him, disciplined him and finally loved him with all his heart.

Perhaps his grandfather's advanced years, coupled with Stefano having come to know him so late in the old man's life, explained why he didn't have what Jack called "the Mafia thing" in his blood. His grandfather never told him tales of bloodshed and revenge. He told him, instead, of *La Sicilia,* of *Castello Lucchesi,* of the cliffs and the volcano and the sea.

Those were the things that beat in Stefano's blood, the things he cherished without ever having seen them.

It was only on his deathbed that the old man motioned him close, whispered of honor and pride and *famiglia,* of how he'd had to abandon everything and come to America to save what he could: Stefano's father and, by extension, Stefano.

"I will get it all back," Stefano had vowed.

It took time. Years to work his way through college, though by his senior year, he was impatient. During summer internships, he'd learned to hate the falseness of the corporate life that had been his goal, to despise the "old boy" network that was already working to deny him entry, the handshake that often accompanied the knife in the back.

His college roommate felt the same way. TJ was into computers. In those days, billionaires were made overnight in Internet start-up companies. TJ was going to be one of those billionaires. He had a great idea, he had the skill, the vision…

All he needed was the money.

One winter day, his hard-earned next semester's tuition in hand, Stefano climbed into his ancient VW, headed toward Yale—and kept on going north, to a casino where he bought into a game of high-stakes poker. It was the first unplanned thing he'd ever done since the day he'd promised his grandfather to win back the Lucchesi honor, but he didn't let himself think about that.

He told himself he deserved a day off. He was a good poker player; he played for fun in school. In fact, he'd won his old VW at a poker table at a middle of the night game in his college dorm, when another guy thought he'd been bluffing with a flush showing on the table.

That day at the casino, Stefano won more than a VW. He won thousands of dollars.

The casino gave him a free room. He staggered to it, showered, slept, ate and returned to the table. Three days later, he drove back to school, dumped a small fortune on his surprised roommate's bed and watched TJ stare at the bills in disbelief.

"Whadja do, man, rob a bank?"

"There's your start-up investment," Stefano said. "I want fifty-one percent control."

A muscle jerked in Stefano's jaw. Fast-forward a dozen years.

The start-up had made him wealthy beyond his wildest dreams. Now, even though his money was invested in aerospace companies, in Texas oil, in luxury condos in Manhattan, he'd never forgotten the pledge he'd made his grandfather.

Two years ago, he'd set out to fulfill it, but it had taken the conversation with his attorney to remind him that there were places and people where ancient vendettas still made the blood hot with rage.

The hot sirocco wind beat at Stefano's back, whipping his dark hair around his lean face. He pushed the strands back and again tucked his hands into the pockets of his jeans.

"Double our initial offer," he'd instructed his attorney.

"That's far too much money. The land isn't worth—"

"No, but their pride is. Make the offer, and make it clear that I have my pride to consider, too. Tell them I'm making them an offer they can't refuse."

Jack had met the statement with a long silence. At last, he'd cleared his throat.

"You watched those movies, huh?"

Stefano had laughed. "Just make the offer and get back to me."

Now it was done. All this—the land, the cliffs, what remained of the *castello* and the view that stretched on forever—was his. So was the house he'd built, just beyond the ruins. He'd had the architect blend it into the rugged scenery and use stones from the original castle. The result was a handsome home, high-ceilinged, with walls of glass that looked over the volcano and the sea.

Stefano smiled. His grandfather, he was certain, would have been pleased.

Tonight, just after moonrise, he'd come out here again with a bottle of *moscato* and a glass. He'd pour the wine, lift the glass to the sea and toast the spirit of all those who'd come and gone before him.

And he would try to keep this place invisible to the rest of the world.

If the tabloids got word, they'd have a field day with what he'd done. It would put a sexy spin on the gossip that already swirled around him. He was building an empire, they said. He was a man of mystery. He was *uno lupo solo*. A lone wolf.

They were right about that, at least. Lucchesi Enterprises had made Stefano a public figure. Because of it, he cherished seclusion in his day-to-day life.

He'd followed his usual practice in building his new house, hiring only those who agreed to sign contracts that contained confidentiality clauses, making it clear his lawyers would be merciless in enforcing those clauses. Word would get out eventually, he knew, but this would give him some breathing room.

A little while ago, a helicopter had buzzed overhead. There was nothing unusual in that; helicopters were part of the twenty-first century. Still, he'd looked up, wondering if somehow the paparazzi had already caught up with him.

"Stef-an-oh."

Stefano caught his breath. Was it the wind? The sound of that voice, calling his name. No. It had to be the wind.

"*Stef-annn-oh*. Yoo-hoo. Don't you hear me?"

He blinked. The wind couldn't put words into sentences, couldn't paint the slender figure of a woman looking up at him from the foot of the hill, one hand scooping back her blond hair, the other cupping her mouth.

Carla? His heart thudded. It couldn't be. She was in New York. He'd left her there one morning last week, tears trailing down her perfectly made-up face, stopping when she realized he meant every word, her voice rising to a shriek as she told him what she thought of him.

The trouble had started when she burst into his apartment without warning and found him sitting at the dining room table, drinking coffee and looking at photos of the island: the windswept cliffs, the old ruins and the new house.

"Omygod," she'd said breathlessly, "darling, what is this?"

There'd been no sense in saying he didn't know. The architect had put together a handsome final portfolio, and each photo was neatly labeled.

Castello Lucchesi, Sicily.

"A house," he'd said indifferently, as if that were all there was to it.

"Your house," she'd said, in that breathless way he'd once found charming and now found irritating. "And it's perfect for the cover of the premiere issue of *Bridal Dreams.*"

"No."

"Now, Stefano," she'd said, slipping into his lap, "you know I was hired to make *Bridal Dreams* the best magazine in the world. The first issue can make me or break me."

No, he'd said again, and she'd changed tack, twisted around so she was straddling him, put her hot mouth to his.

He should have thrown her out right then. Their relationship had grown stale; it was over and he knew it. He'd lost interest in Carla—she was self-centered and superficial, and she wanted things he had no intention of giving her—a place in his life, a future with him.

He'd been with a dozen women who'd wanted the same things and he was no more interested in permanent commitment to Carla than he'd been with the others. Carla had known that, going in; she said her life was her career, but somewhere along the way, she'd decided to change her game plan.

So he'd lifted her from his lap, told her "No" again, and as she began to weep, his phone rang. It was his pilot, saying his Learjet had been serviced and was ready whenever he was.

"Where are you going?" Carla cried as he started for the door. "You have to do this for me, Stefano. You have to!"

When he didn't answer, she'd gone from crying to cursing and screaming...

And now she was here. On his land. His island. Scrambling up the hill toward him like something out of a bad dream.

He felt his insides knot into a ball of fury at her temerity in violating this place. He told himself he was being ridiculous, that this wasn't a shrine. The only thing he had the right to be angry about was that she'd followed him on this trip without being invited, but that didn't keep him from jamming his hands even harder into his pockets and balling them into fists.

"Darling," she squealed as she reached him. "Aren't you surprised to see me?"

"How did you find me?" he said curtly.

"That's not much of a hello."

"You're right. It's a question. Please answer it."

She smiled as she rose on tiptoe and pressed a kiss to his unmoving mouth.

"It wasn't that difficult. I'm sure you think I have a bubble for a brain, but even a child could have—"

"I'm sorry you made such a long journey for nothing, Carla."

"Is that all you have to say to me after I've come so far to be with you?"

His mouth twisted. She had come for her own reasons. Being with him had nothing to do with it. He knew that, and she knew he knew it.

"—such a magnificent place, darling, and to think you didn't intend to share it with—"

"Was that helicopter yours?"

"Yes. Yes, it was. It landed in a field just a little way from here and then a taxi—"

"Go back to it and tell the pilot to take you back to the airport."

Carla blinked. "What?"

"I said—"

"I heard you. I just can't believe you'd send me away."

Tears glinted in her eyes. She was good at this, he thought grimly. Very good.

"Carla." He spoke quietly, feeling the anger inside him approaching critical mass and determined not to let her know it. He valued self-control as much as privacy. Explosive emotion was the one thing Sicilian he didn't admire. It had led his grandfather to ruin. "You're not staying here."

"You mean…" Her mouth trembled. "You mean, I'm not welcome."

He almost laughed. Did she really think a show of injured feelings would work?

"I mean," he said carefully, "I didn't invite you."

"You didn't have to. We've been together a long time."

"Four months." His voice turned cold. He knew it, but all at once, he didn't care.

"Four months," she repeated, making it sound like a

lifetime, "and now, just because I asked you a simple favor—"

"I gave you a simple answer. No one is putting my home on the cover of a magazine."

"Then, it *is* your home?" she said with a sly little smile. "You're not developing this property into a resort?"

Stefano cursed himself for being a fool. "Goodbye, Carla," he said, and started past her.

She reached out and caught his sleeve.

"I don't want it for a cover, Stefano. I want it for the entire issue."

He laughed.

"It'll be the most incredible magazine anyone's ever seen!" He tugged his arm free of her hand and began walking down the slope. Carla hurried alongside him, slipping a little in her stiletto heels. "Just listen, okay?"

He didn't answer.

"The way I've planned things will protect your precious privacy as much as it heightens the intimacy of the shoot."

They reached the bottom of the hill. Stefano looked around for her taxi. The road and the driveway were empty.

"Here's my plan, Stefano." Carla moved in front of him, face glowing under the soft lights that had just come on in the rear of the house. "One of everything. One world-class photographer, one incredible makeup artist, one unbelievably gorgeous model—"

She cried out as he cupped her elbows and hauled her to her toes.

"No! Are you deaf? There will be no shoot. No model, no photographer, no anything."

"You're hurting me."

He probably was. Carefully, he took his hands from her and stepped back.

"Where's your cab?"

"I sent it back." She smiled. "I sent the helicopter back, too."

"Wait here. I'll have someone drive you to the airport," he said, and walked away from her for what would surely be the last time.

"Stefano."

Her voice was soft; it held something that made the hair rise on the back of his neck, but he kept going.

"Which magazine would you rather see these photos in, *Bridal Dreams*...or *Whispers*?"

He came to an abrupt stop.

"You have a minute to reconsider that threat," he said as he swung toward her, "and then I'm going to pick you up and throw you off my land."

Carla's face was white. She was frightened. But she was determined, too. He could see it in the tilt of her head.

"I've already made all the arrangements. The model, the makeup man, the photographer... They'll all be here tomorrow."

He felt his jaw drop. Dimly, in a part of his mind that was observing all this with dry curiosity, he wondered what the world would think if it knew that one sentence, spoken by one woman, could have such an effect on *il lupo solo*.

"Excuse me?"

"I said—"

He moved quickly, grabbed her by the shoulders and shook her until her teeth rattled.

"What the hell are you talking about?"

"Let go!"

"Damn you, explain yourself!"

"I'll sue you for assault if you don't let go!"

It wouldn't be assault, it would be murder. He was a heartbeat away from it. Stunned by the intensity of his rage, he let her go.

"Explain yourself."

"I did, but you wouldn't listen." She wrapped her arms

around herself and looked up at him. Her voice took on timbre; excitement flashed in her eyes. "You think you know all about making money? Maybe, but you don't know squat about magazine publishing. You debut a new magazine or relaunch an old one, what you need is to produce an issue that'll set the country talking. Just one issue, and the magazine will be so hot it'll sizzle. And so will I."

"Sizzle some other way. No one is setting foot here without my permission."

"We'll be here three days, no more than that. I won't insult you by offering you money for the right to do the shoot here."

He laughed, and her cheeks reddened.

"Don't make me force your hand, darling."

"Force it?" he said through his teeth.

"You want to keep your life a deep, dark mystery, don't you?" She smiled slyly. "Offhand, I can think of half a dozen tabloids that would love an exclusive interview with the great Stefano Lucchesi's mistress—along with aerial photos of his new hideaway."

In the ensuing silence, Stefano could hear everything. The pound of his heart. The distant boom of the surf and the sharp cry of a bird far over the rolling sea. He could feel the shadows behind him, the ghosts of the wild warriors who'd done whatever was necessary to protect this place.

"I could kill you," he said softly. "No one would know. All I have to do is drag you to the top of the cliff and throw you off. By the time your remains washed up, the crabs would have eaten their fill."

Carla's smile trembled but she moved closer to him.

"You're a heartless bastard when you want to be, Stefano Lucchesi, but killing women? Never."

Stefano stared at his former lover for long moments. Then he spat at her feet, brushed past her and headed for the house.

So much for his dreams.

She had defiled this place.

Maybe his grandfather had been wise to have left the island behind.

CHAPTER TWO

ALL the oceans of the world looked the same from 35,000 feet…and wasn't it sad when you'd flown so often that you could think of nothing but that when you were almost seven miles above the Atlantic?

Fallon O'Connell sat back, pressed the button that fully reclined her soft leather seat and wondered when she'd turned into such a world-weary cynic.

Across the aisle, a little boy traveling with his mother sat with his nose almost pressed to the glass, enthralled by the cloudless view of the ocean miles below and by the wonder of leaving Connecticut this evening and arriving in Italy tomorrow morning…but then, the kid hadn't made this trip a million times.

She'd been as excited as he was, her first flight to Europe ten years ago.

Fallon closed her eyes.

She was on her way to an island in the Mediterranean for a one week shoot, a suite in a mansion waiting for her as well as the best makeup artist and cameraman in the business ready to work their magic…

Her mouth twitched.

A little enthusiasm might be a good idea right about now.

She sighed, sat up straight and peered out the window again.

It wasn't that she didn't want the job. What model wouldn't? The inaugural cover of *Bridal Dreams* and inside it, pages and pages of glossy photographs devoted to her.

Of course, she wanted it.

So, what was the problem? That was what her brother Cullen had asked her last night, after Keir's and Cassie's wedding.

The newlyweds had finally made their laughing escape, but the O'Connell clan wasn't finished celebrating. They'd moved the festivities from the lushness of the Tender Grapes restaurant up to the handsome stone house that overlooked Deer Hill Vineyard.

Sean lit a fire on the massive hearth.

Anybody want to roast an ox? he'd said, to much laughter.

Cullen opened another bottle of Deer Hill's prize-winning Chardonnay.

Damn good thing Keir bought himself a vineyard instead of a soft drink franchise, he'd said, to more laughter.

Cullen filled all their glasses. Sean went through Keir's collection of CDs and put on something soft and classical while their mother and stepfather settled on the sofa. Megan, Briana and Fallon kicked off their stiletto heels and groaned with pleasure.

How about taking the dollar tour? Bree said.

Yeah, Megan answered, looping her arm through Bree's. *Maybe we can finally figure out how many rooms this place really has.*

She held out a hand to Fallon, but Fallon smiled and shook her head.

"You guys go ahead. I'm going to step outside for a breath of air."

Her sisters trooped off and Cullen looked over at her. "You okay?"

"I'm fine," she said, flashing another smile. "I just want to take a look at the sky. I'm not used to seeing all these stars."

Her brother grinned. ''Me, neither. Us city types tend to forget.''

Fallon nodded, opened the sliding glass doors and stepped out on the terrace. The stars shone down with crystalline brilliance from a black-velvet sky; the ivory moon seemed caught in the uplifted branches of a stand of trees.

The warm air of the Connecticut summer night enveloped her.

Wineglass in hand, Fallon went down stone steps that still held some of the day's heat. She made her way slowly along the gentle slope of the hill and through terraced rows of grapevines.

There, the earth was cool and moist against her bare feet—she and her sisters had decided to forgo panty hose under their long bridesmaids' gowns. The breeze, perfumed by heavy clusters of ripening grapes, smelled delicious.

It had been a lovely day. A wonderful weekend. Her mother was blissfully happy with Dan, who'd turned out to be the kind of stepfather that gave the word luster. Spending time with her sisters and brothers was always fun, and her oldest brother was so crazy in love with his Cassie that it almost made you believe in love.

For someone else, at least, if not for yourself.

Fallon stopped walking, sipped some of the wine, ran a hand lightly over a cluster of velvety grapes.

Then, how come she was feeling so—so—

What? What *was* she feeling? Weary? Under the weather? Maybe even a little bit down? There was no reason for it, none at—

''Hey.''

She gasped and spun around just as Cullen reached her.

''You scared me to half to death,'' she said with a little laugh.

''Sorry. I figured you heard me coming.'' He grinned. ''I guess I have a delicate walk.''

Fallon grinned back at him. "Delicate" was not a word anyone would use to describe her brothers. Cullen, like the rest of them, was big, six foot two in his stockinged feet.

"Uh-huh. About as delicate as a moose. What are you doing out here?"

Cullen shrugged. "Same as you, kid. Checking the stars, stretching my legs, taking a breather. It's been a long day."

"A long weekend, you mean. Fun, though."

"The gathering of the O'Connell clan always is. Fewer fireworks than usual this time, at least."

Fallon laughed. "Probably out of deference to Cassie. I guess none of us wanted to scare her off. She scored lots of points, being able to tolerate all of us at one clip."

"Uh-huh. She seems terrific."

"I agree."

Brother and sister sipped their wine.

"Amazing," Cullen said, after a while. "That Keir got married, I mean."

"It happens," Fallon said lightly.

"Sure, but not to us." They both laughed. "It was a great ceremony."

"Mmm."

"Those vows they wrote were cool."

"Mmm," Fallon said again, and took another sip of wine.

"Touching."

Her eyebrows rose. "Touching?"

"Yeah. You know, the sentiments they expressed. Isn't a man permitted to use the word? You thought so, too."

Fallon blinked. "Were we talking about me?"

Cullen, who'd hours ago discarded his tuxedo jacket and bow tie, opened the top buttons of his shirt.

"You cried a little," he said softly. "At the end."

"Me? Cry at a wedding?" Fallon turned toward him

and poked a finger into the middle of his chest. "Cullen. My darling little brother—"

"You're only a year older than I am, kid. Don't let it go to your head."

"The point is, I do not cry at weddings. Why would I? When you've been a bride nine trillion times—"

"A magazine-cover bride, six times, and don't look so surprised. Ma keeps count."

Fallon looked up at him. "Does she?"

"Damned right. And if you want to know the rest, she sends each of us a copy of every magazine that has you on the cover... As if we all didn't run to the nearest store and buy up all the copies ourselves."

Pleased beyond reason, Fallon smiled.

"That's nice."

"Nice? It's necessary. How do you think those magazines stay in circulation? If the O'Connells didn't buy 'em, who would?" He laughed, ducked away from the fist his sister teasingly aimed at his jaw. "But being a bride on a cover doesn't make you a bride in real life, babe. We both know that."

Fallon narrowed her eyes. "What's happening here? You think, now that Keir's gone down the aisle, we all should?"

Cullen shuddered. "Hell, no!"

"Good. Because I'm not the least bit interested in getting married."

"Fine with me. I'm just wondering why you were crying." His voice gentled. "You okay?"

"Of course I'm okay. Why wouldn't I be?"

"I don't know. That's why I'm asking. If some guy out there hurt you or something—"

"Oh, Cull," Fallon said softly. Her lips curved in a smile; she clasped her brother's forearms, lifted to her toes and kissed him on the cheek. "Thank you."

"Hey, did I or did I not beat up Billy Buchanan for you in fifth grade, when he wrote 'I Luv Amy' on that fence instead of 'I Luv Fallon' after he'd sworn to be your boyfriend forever?''

Fallon grinned. ''Probably because he couldn't spell Fallon, but yes, you did.''

''Well, any other SOB gives you a bad time, you tell me, okay?''

She stared at Cullen, wondering what he'd say if he knew that she didn't even date anymore, that one man too many had coveted her as a trophy to be won and ignored her as a woman who wanted to be loved for who she was, not what she was.

''Sis?''

Fallon smiled and looped her arm through his. ''Okay.''

They began walking up the hill, toward the turreted stone house illuminated by moonlight.

''It was just that it all seemed so—so right,'' she said after a minute, her voice soft and low. ''The flowers. The words. The music. The way Keir and Cassie looked at each other. I guess you're right. It was touching.''

''Sure.''

''Not that I want any of it for myself.''

''Your career,'' Cullen said, nodding as if he understood that there was no room in her life for anything else.

Except, how could he understand when she didn't? After years of hard work, her career was at its peak...and she wasn't enjoying it half as much as she'd expected.

She'd hit it big at seventeen, just walking along a New York street on a break between finishing high school and starting college. A man had come up to her, shoved his card at her, said, when she jerked back, that he wasn't a child molester or a lunatic, that he owned a modeling agency and if she wasn't a fool, she'd come in to talk with him.

Fallon had never been a fool. You didn't get to be valedictorian of your class or survive a childhood spent moving from place to place by being stupid. She'd checked out the name of the agency, called for an appointment and met with the man who now bore the distinction of having discovered her.

By the time she was eighteen, her face was everywhere. So was she. A week in Spain, another in Paris, long weekends in the Caribbean and on Florida's Gold Coast that very first year, and scores of places ever since.

Maybe that was why she'd been so emotional yesterday, at the wedding. Maybe it was knowing that Keir and Cassie were going to put down roots.

Maybe it was why she was staring out the jet's window again, wondering when she'd realized that one ocean was like another, one island like another, one man like another—

"Miss O'Connell?"

Fallon looked up. The cabin attendant was standing over her, smiling and offering the breakfast menu. She shook her head, declined everything but a small pot of coffee.

When it came, she raised her seat halfway and poured a cup.

You had to watch your weight when you modeled, more and more as the years sped by. The svelte figure you had at eighteen wasn't the same as the one you had at twenty-eight.

Twenty-eight, she thought, sipping at the hot black coffee. Pushing thirty. Not bad in this business. Her body was still all right; hours in the gym kept it that way, but she'd have to do some things to her face soon, if she wanted to keep going. Maybe get her eyelids done or her mouth plumped with collagen. Take a shot of Botox to keep wrinkles from between her brows.

She hated even the thought of doing something so artificial. As it was, there were times she looked in the mirror after someone had done her hair and her face, after someone else had chosen what she would wear, after still another person told her to look soulful or excited or whatever would sell cars or hand lotion, and wondered who she was.

Surgery, injections, little tucks and snips would only make the real Fallon more difficult to find.

Sometimes, she looked in the mirror and wondered what life would be like if she were a real person instead of a woman created by the camera.

Fallon grimaced and put down her cup.

For heaven's sake, what was wrong with her?

She was Fallon O'Connell, supermodel. Thousands of women would give anything to trade places with her, and every last one of them would tell her she was certifiably crazy not to be happy.

She had a wonderful, exciting life. And she knew, even if nobody else except her family did, that she was more than just a pretty face.

She smiled, remembering the way Sean and Cullen had greeted her at the Hartford airport a few days ago, enfolding her in rib-squeezing hugs, Sean saying he was glad to see she was still as homely as sin, Cullen adding yes, it was true, and wasn't it a terrible shame?

Fallon chuckled. Her family knew how to keep her grounded.

She pressed the seat button and sat up straight.

Enough of this silliness. She had to concentrate on the job ahead. It was an incredible assignment. She'd be the only model in the shoot, and she'd work with Maurice, her favorite photographer, and Andy, a genius of a makeup artist who'd always been able to make her look ethereal.

Carla—the *Bridal Dreams* editor who'd set up the whole thing—would be there, too, but that was it. Just their little group, and nobody else, not even the mansion's owner. That was a relief. She'd done shoots on private property before and sometimes the owners got so starstruck and excited, they got in the way.

Not this time.

This owner, Carla said, was an old man with a bad temper. God only knew what magic Carla had worked to convince him to let them use the site for the shoot. When Fallon had asked, Carla winked and said it was a secret. She'd probably used that same magic to get the old guy out of the way. Carla said she'd given him the option of staying around but he'd refused.

So there'd be just a handful of people, people Fallon already knew, and the ruins of an old castle, a view Carla swore went on forever, the sun, the sea, the beach...

And the volcano, smoldering in the distance.

She felt better, just imagining it.

She'd been to Sicily before, only for a couple of days. That had been work, too, but she'd been one of three models. The other girls had hated the island. They said it was too rugged, too old-world, too windswept, but Fallon had loved it.

Sicily was reality. Islands where the trees were lush, the land gently rolling, the people smiling and laid-back were fantasies.

A touch of reality was a breath of fresh air in a life where the end product was illusion.

The sound of the jet's engines changed. It was subtle, but she'd flown enough to recognize the different nuances in tone. The pilot was throttling back. Soon, he'd put down the flaps and lower the landing gear.

Fallon leaned toward the window. The sky was turning light; a slender red thread stretched across the horizon. They'd be over land any minute, touching down in Paris where she'd change planes for the last leg of her flight.

Perhaps, she thought with a little kick of excitement, perhaps Sicily was where she'd finally figure out who she was and what she was going to do with the rest of her life, because the truth was, the future was on her mind lately.

On her mind, a lot.

Fallon shut her eyes, blocked out the sound of the engines and the excited voice of the little boy across the aisle. She took a deep breath, held it, then exhaled slowly and deeply.

A couple of relaxation exercises, she'd be absolutely fine.

A few hours later, not even a day's worth of relaxation exercises would have helped calm her nerves.

What kind of place was this?

Was there supposed to be a deluge in Catania at this time of year? Was she supposed to be so wet and cold that she was shivering?

Plus, nobody spoke English. Well, nobody here at the cab stand. Nobody spoke Italian, either. Fallon did, a little. More than a little; she had a good ear and she'd picked up a considerable amount of the language when she lived in Milan for six weeks at the start of her career.

What people were talking here sounded like Italian, but it wasn't. It was a dialect, sort of what you heard in New York when you went into one of those fantastic little shops all the way downtown where they said "proh-voh-lone" when they meant "prah-vah-lohn-eh" or "scun-geel" when they meant "scun-gee-lee."

You thought you understood. And you did. Almost. But there was a huge difference between clarifying things by smiling and pointing at a chunk of cheese or a tray of octopus and trying to figure out how to ask if this was or was not the place to wait for a private car that was supposed to come for you.

Fallon shoved a wet hank of hair from her eyes.

Where the hell was her ride?

Her flight had come in on time. She'd collected her luggage, gone through customs, headed out the door absolutely according to Carla's directions…

And waited.

And waited.

And waited some more, without the protection of an

umbrella or a raincoat, just a thin cotton jacket over an even thinner T-shirt and cotton slacks.

Where was that miserable car?

She darted out from the wretched protection of an overhang and checked the road again, searching for a car that looked as if its driver might be searching for *her*.

Fiats and Alfa-Romeos went by. And taxis, lots of taxis, and, damn it, she'd have taken one if she knew where she was going but she didn't have the address. Why would she have needed it, when a car was picking her up?

Fallon dashed back to the wall, soaked to the skin, her hair dripping down her back and in her eyes, her clothes plastered to her body.

Maurice, the photographer, and Andy, the makeup guy, had flown over yesterday with Carla. She'd had to come a day late because of the wedding. No doubt the three of them were sitting in that castle, warm and dry, drinking *vino* while she stood here and drowned.

Okay. To hell with waiting for a driver who wasn't coming. She'd go into the terminal, find a phone, call the *Bridal Dreams* office…

And reach nobody. It was the beginning of the day here, which meant it was still the middle of the night in New York.

"Damn," she said under her breath, "damn, damn!"

A big black car pulled out of the line of traffic and turned toward the curb. Fallon held her breath. Was the driver looking for her? She couldn't see him; the windows were darkly tinted and the rain was coming down in sheets, but yes, the car was stopping, the driver was getting out, going around the car, opening the door…

Fallon raced to the car and tossed her suitcase inside.

The driver looked startled. *"Signorina. Uno momento!"*

"It's okay," she gasped, "you don't have to put the case in the trunk. Just let me get inside where it's dry."

''By all means,'' a deep, amused voice said. ''Any port will do in a storm.''

A man was sitting in the shadowed corner of the back seat, smiling at her.

Fallon's first thought was that he was gorgeous. Dark hair, heavily-lashed dark eyes, a classical Roman nose…

Her second was that this couldn't possibly be her car if someone was already inside it.

Her third was that she was out of the wet and the cold for the first time in almost half an hour.

She cleared her throat. ''I don't suppose… Is there the slightest possibility someone sent you to meet me?''

The man grinned. ''I'd love to say yes but, regretfully, I have to say that nobody sent me to meet you.''

''Ah.'' Still crouched just inside the car, Fallon put her hand to her hair and shoved the sodden mass from her face. ''Well, then, I'm sorry to have bothered you. I mean, I've been waiting for a car that was supposed to come for me, and—''

''How about fate?''

''Excuse me?''

''Would it be all right if I said fate sent me to meet you?''

Oh, yes. Definitely gorgeous, and with a smooth line.

''Unfortunately,'' she answered, with a quick smile, ''fate's not going to take me where I'm going.'' Still smiling, she started scooting backward. ''Again, my apologies for—''

''My driver can take you wherever you're going.''

She blinked. Stefano knew he'd surprised her with his offer. Hell, he'd surprised himself, too.

What was he doing, telling a strange woman she could use his car to take her wherever it was she was going? On the other hand, she was a delectable stranger, even as wet as she was. Even? Stefano let his gaze drop to her breasts, their roundness, their tight little nipples perfectly outlined under her clinging shirt.

If anything, the rain heightened her beauty.

He felt a quick stir in his loins, a sudden surge of hunger that shocked him with its intensity. He hadn't felt this kind of desire since his breakup with Carla. Actually, not for weeks before that.

"That's very generous of you, *signore,* but I can't accept."

His eyes lifted to hers. Her face was a little flushed, as if she'd noticed the way he'd looked at her. She was shivering, which made sense considering how wet she was, and Stefano cursed himself for evaluating her sexually at such a moment.

"Of course you can. I'm getting out here and my driver has nowhere to go after he leaves me. He can take you to your hotel."

Fallon shook her head. "That's just it. I'm not going to a hotel. I—"

"The rain's coming in. Why don't you sit down, let Luigi shut the door and turn on some heat while we discuss this."

She hesitated. He knew she had to be weighing the pros and cons of the situation. Should a woman get into a car with a stranger or not?

He smiled.

"You're American."

"Yes."

"Well, so am I. That makes us kindred souls. What's the title of that old book? *Strangers in a Strange Land.*"

"Heinlein," she said, with a delighted smile, and that seemed to do it. The woman bounced onto the leather seat beside him, shoved her hair back from her face and held out her hand. "Fallon O'Connell," she said, but when he reached for her hand she laughed, drew it back, wiped the wetness on her trouser leg before holding it out again. "I'm soaked."

"So you are."

Stefano smiled as he clasped her hand in his. God, she

was beautiful! Who was she visiting in Sicily? A man? He felt an irrational surge of jealousy for some faceless stranger. Maybe she wasn't visiting a man. Maybe he ought to stay on the island instead of returning to New York and celebrate his newfound freedom.

"And your name is…?"

He laughed. "Sorry. I'm Stefano Lucchesi. It's very nice to meet you, Miss O'Connell."

"Fallon, please. It's nice to meet you, too, Mr.—"

"Stefano." He let go of her hand, though he really didn't want to, sat back and folded his arms. "Now that we've been formally introduced, tell me why you can't let my driver take you to your destination."

"You'll think I'm crazy."

"I doubt that."

"Well, you see, I don't know the address."

Stefano grinned. "A mystery vacation?"

She laughed. She had a great laugh, light and musical and real.

"I wish. I'm not on vacation at all."

"Ah. Don't tell me. You're the American sales rep for Lamborghini."

She laughed again, and he thought how nice it was to be able to make her eyes crinkle up that way.

"I'm here on assignment for a magazine, but the person who hired me didn't give me an address. It didn't seem necessary, because she said she'd have a car pick me up."

Stefano felt his smile tilt. "*She* said?"

"Yes."

He drew a deep breath. "I don't suppose you're a model, Miss O'Connell."

"It's Fallon, remember? And yes, I am. Did you just recognize me?"

She said it with a smile but there was disappointment in her eyes. Why? he wondered. Because he hadn't recognized her sooner? Yes, that would be the reason. He knew the kind of woman she was, aware of her looks, trading on them, assuming no man could resist her. And he, like a fool, had been busy proving her right.

Until now.

She was connected to Carla, a part of Carla's plan to violate his sanctuary. And he wanted nothing to do with her.

"No," he said curtly, "I didn't recognize you."

"Oh. Then, how—"

"There's talk all over the island of the idiots who are going to take foolish pictures for a useless magazine."

It was a lie. There'd been no talk. Carla had kept to the bargain; she'd been discreet and he'd surely told no one, but it was as good an excuse as any. He was angry, angrier than he had the right to be, and for no good reason. What Fallon O'Connell did for a living was her affair, not his.

Apparently, she thought so, too. Her smile vanished; that lovely face turned cool.

"I don't consider my occupation useless, Mr. Lucchesi."

"My apologies," he said in a way that made a mockery of the words. She knew it, too, because color swept into her cheeks.

"You don't know anything about my profession, mister! The pictures will be beautiful, and thousands of readers would tell you how much the articles in the magazine—"

"I'm sure they would," he said, cutting her short, "but then, there's no accounting for bad taste."

Just for a second, he thought she was going to slug him. The thought had a certain appeal. Her hand swinging in an arc, his reaching out to stop her, grabbing her by the shoulders, pulling her against him and crushing that lush mouth beneath his until her indignation became desire...

Damn it, was he crazy?

"Okay." Her voice was low and trembling with repressed anger. "That's enough."

She reached for the door; he caught her hand to stop her and felt a bolt of electricity shoot from her fingers to his before she jerked back.

"How you earn your living is your affair. The point is, I know the place you want." He leaned forward and tapped his driver's shoulder. "Luigi. The lady wants to go to the *castello*. Take her there."

"I'd rather walk than accept a favor from you."

"Don't be a fool. How can you go someplace if you don't know its location?"

"Just tell me where it is and we'll call it even."

"My driver will take you."

"Damn it, are you deaf? I don't want to spend another minute in this car!"

"It isn't the car, it's me."

Her eyes flashed. Soaked to the skin, as disheveled as a wet cat, she still had a presence about her.

"You've got that right!"

"In that case…" Stefano wrenched the door open, stepped into the road and slammed the door shut. "*Arrivederci*, Miss O'Connell. Luigi?" He slapped the side of the car. "*Andante.*"

Fallon O'Connell said something to him. He couldn't hear it but this close to the smoked glass window, he could see her mouth open in angry indignation.

Whatever it was, he suspected it wasn't polite.

She reached for the door and he slapped the car again. Luigi, ever obedient, discreetly activated the door locks and floored the gas pedal.

The car shot away from the curb.

Stefano strode into the terminal, got halfway through it and stopped. What the hell was he doing? He cursed under his breath, an eloquent, earthy string of Sicilian that would have made his grandfather proud as he took his cell phone from his pocket and called his pilot.

"Change of plans," he said briskly. "We're not going

anywhere today. In fact, you might as well take the next few days off. I'll be staying in Sicily for a while.''

Of course he'd stay, he thought grimly as he hurried back to the taxi stand. What had he been thinking, to risk leaving the *castello* while Carla and her people were there?

She had instructions. So did his house staff. None of the *Bridal Dreams* people were to be permitted past the door. Carla had been upset; where would she put her little crew? she'd said. She'd already told them they'd be staying in the castle.

Untell them, he'd said coldly.

For all he gave a damn, she could put them in sleeping bags on the rocky beach, but there was an inn a few miles away and that was where she'd arranged they'd spend the week.

He'd checked to make sure she'd really made the reservations, and he'd pushed up the installation of a full security system for the *castello* by a couple of months. He'd even gone a step further and arranged for around-the-clock security people to patrol the grounds.

"Taxi, *signore?*"

Stefano nodded, handed over a few bills and climbed into the cab.

"*Il Castello Lucchesi,*" he said.

Still, how could he be sure his orders were followed unless he was there?

He'd been stupid to leave his home while strangers were on the property. Going back was the only way to safeguard his privacy.

An image flashed before him of the woman he'd just met, her eyes wide and mysterious, her mouth warm and sensual. For an instant, he thought he could smell her scent, an innocent breath of vanilla that only accentuated the lushness of her beauty.

Stefano's mouth thinned.

He wasn't doing this because of Fallon O'Connell. He was doing it because it was logical.

There was no other reason.

None at all.

CHAPTER THREE

A TRAVEL magazine would have dubbed the Lucchesi Estate magnificent.

The setting was spectacular. Tall cypresses flanked the ancient ruins that had once been a medieval castle. It backed against a cliff that fell away to the deep blue Mediterranean, and faced the slumbering volcano called Mount Etna.

On the same plateau, probably where the ancient out-buildings of the castle had once sprawled, stood a modern castle, a structure that was all cool smoked glass and native stone. There was a terrace behind it, a garden surrounding that, and off by itself, a free-form pool with an infinity edge that made it seem as if the water in the pool fell straight down the cliff, into the sea.

Beautiful, all of it…and after almost a week, Fallon hoped to God she'd never set eyes on the place again.

The sun was merciless, blazing down like golden fire from a sky so blue it seemed artificial. Shooting on the terrace hour after hour, with the sea at her back, meant she spent most of her time staring at the castle and all that dark glass. It was like looking at someone wearing mirrored sunglasses. Were they watching you, or was it your imagination? It was always impossible to tell.

Filming in the pool was better, but Maurice thought that setting too tame. He preferred the beach, and that was hell.

The beach was rocky, the stones hot and sharp beneath her bare feet, and even when Maurice motioned her into the surf, the water was tepid against her ankles and calves rather than cooling.

The last day of the shoot seemed endless. Maurice was barking out orders, as usual.

"Angle toward me! Get that arm back! Think sexy!"

Think sexy? All she could think was thirsty, but she moistened her lips, turned a half smile to the camera and clung to the thought that they'd be finished in just another few minutes.

She was hot; her feet were raw from the rocks and her skin was itchy under its layer of sunscreen. Andy had used waterproof makeup on her face and it felt like a mask, and the hairdresser—Carla had brought along more than the three people she'd promised—the hairdresser had sprayed so much gunk at her head that she felt like she was wearing a wig.

"Let's go, O'Connell! This time, run into the surf. Look like you're having a good time. Give me lots of splash."

The only thing she wanted to give him was a sock in the jaw. But she was a pro; she knew how to do her job. And she was trying to do it, she really was. It was just that she'd come here expecting to love this place.

Instead, she hated it.

"Smile. Yes. That's it. Another one, over your shoulder this time."

The sun, reflecting off the sea in sparkling flashes, was too bright. She had a headache from it by the end of each day. The beach was impossible to walk on, all those stones cutting into the tender soles of her feet.

"Okay, honey. Drape yourself over the big rock. You know what I want, babe. Lean back on your hands. Nice. Very nice. Bigger smile. Yeah, like that. Good, fine— except turn your head. Give me the look. You know the one. That's it. Nice. Very nice. Now you're cookin'."

Cooking was the word. This place could pass for hell's anteroom. Had it been this hot last time she was in Sicily?

"Go a little farther into the water. Good. Push your hair back. Use both hands—I want to see those tits lift! That's it. Perfect. Now wet your lips and smile.

"O'Connell? Turn around. Try one hand on your hip. Give me a pout. Let your lashes droop. Look at me. You're a bride, you're on your honeymoon, and you're looking at your groom with sex on the brain and nothing else. Pretend you're going to get out of the water soon, go up to that castle and jump his bones. Good. Better. We're getting there."

Go up to that castle? No way. The closest she'd come to it was the day she'd arrived.

The driver had taken her through an imposing gate, past a couple of men with ice for eyes who looked as if they should have been wearing camo and combat boots instead of suits, past security cameras tucked high in the trees, toward a soaring edifice of stone and glass.

"*Il castello,*" the driver said, his voice as solemn as if he were in one of the ancient churches they'd passed on the way.

That he said anything at all startled her. He hadn't spoken a word since they'd left the airport. He didn't understand English, he'd indicated with a lift of his shoulders, but it was a lie.

He'd understood every bloody word his arrogant feudal lord had spoken. It was only when Fallon demanded he let her out of the car that the man suddenly turned mute. She'd ended up shouting at him; she'd come close to reaching over the seat and pummeling his shoulders with frustration.

That wasn't going to happen again.

"How nice," she said coolly.

The truth was, nice didn't come close.

She'd been expecting a medieval structure, cold, gloomy and desolate. This was a soaring mansion that somehow bridged the distance between the past and the present. She craned her neck and stared as they drove past it, until the car came to a gliding stop.

Fallon looked around as the driver got out and opened her door.

They'd stopped beside—

A tent?

"Signorina."

Confused, she looked up at the man. "Are you sure we're in the right place?"

"Si."

She stepped from the car. It was a tent, all right. A big one, true, the kind she'd seen at garden parties in the Hamptons, but a tent just the same.

The driver reached in for her suitcase and at that moment the *Bridal Dreams* crew ran out of the tent to greet her. She hugged Andy and Maurice, exchanged air-kisses with Carla, shook hands with the others and asked the obvious question.

Why were they all hanging around in a tent when there was that big old house just a couple of hundred yards away?

Off-limits, Carla said with a patently false smile. "The owner's eccentric. He doesn't want us using it."

The tent would be their office and dressing room. She'd made catering arrangements for lunch and had a portable john installed in a little cove on the beach.

"It's as if we're camping in the wilderness," Carla said with a gaiety anyone could see was false.

"Don't tell me we're camping here at night, too," Fallon muttered, and Carla laughed and laughed.

"Of course not, darling. We all have rooms at an inn just up the coast. It's a charming little place."

The others, who'd already seen the inn, groaned so that Fallon knew "charming" was a happy euphemism for not enough hot water, lumpy mattresses and threadbare linens.

Carla was the only smart one. She went back to New York on the second day.

Of course, it made for problems, not having Carla on-site. The stylist or the designer's rep or somebody else was almost always clutching a cell phone, talking to New York, asking questions, getting things clarified.

Nobody could figure out why Carla had left. It certainly wasn't the most practical thing to have done but that second morning, Carla's cell phone had rung, she'd answered it, turned white, glanced up in the direction of the big house on the cliff and the next anyone knew, she was gone.

"Important business in New York," she'd said, but Fallon didn't buy it. It just didn't sound right.

Fallon sighed.

Thank goodness the week was almost over.

Tomorrow morning they'd all fly back to the States, and not a moment too soon. Why she'd ever imagined she'd enjoy being on this godforsaken island was a mystery. She'd had enough of the heat, the rocks, the house or mansion or *castello* or whatever it was called looming way up there on the cliff.

She didn't like this place. Nothing about it seemed right, starting on day one when she'd mistaken that big black car at the airport for the one that was supposed to meet her.

That car. That man. Stefano Lucchesi, with the dark and dangerous eyes, the slow smile, the husky, sexy voice.

Ridiculous, how an obnoxious stranger had lodged himself in her mind. She knew the reason: she had zero tolerance for men who thought they owned the world. She'd spent most of the past decade dealing with jerks like that. You damn near tripped over them in every capital on every continent, men who thought that beautiful women were useless and self-indulgent, and that they could be bought or, at least, coerced.

"O'Connell, are you deaf? I said to turn around. Thank you. It's nice to know you're still with us."

Modeling was a strange business. It was full of men

like Maurice, all ego and temperament, and ones like Andy, who were gentle and kind.

And on the periphery were the predators.

Handsome men. Wealthy, powerful men. Men who prowled the clubs where the models danced and drank and relaxed after a day's hard work, who wanted the pleasure that came of wearing stunning arm-candy.

It was, of course, a reciprocal arrangement. The predators got the arm-candy; the girls got the attention, the gifts, the publicity.

Not Fallon. Not since she'd tumbled, hard, for a so-called captain of industry when she was seventeen. She'd given him her heart and her virginity; he'd given her a diamond bracelet and promises, lots of them.

Only the diamond had stood the test of time.

She'd been cautious after that but still, four years later, she'd ended up in a replay of that first relationship. Her lover had been good-looking, rich, notoriously sexy…and he'd given her up when someone new came along.

"O'Connell? Babe, put your hands on your hips, okay? Great. Hold that…"

Her few liaisons since then had been with nice, down-to-earth guys. No I-Am-In-Command egos to deal with. No hunky powerhouses. Nobody to start her pulse pounding excitement at the sight of him, the way it had in that car at the airport when she saw Stefano Lucchesi, saw that beautiful fallen angel's face…

A tremor raced down her spine.

She was definitely glad this project was almost finished. What she needed was the noise and energy of New York. She could deal with the crowds, the traffic, the weather that was always either too hot, too cold or too wet a lot better than she could deal with this place.

She was thinking crazy things, plus her senses were playing tricks on her. For instance, she kept having this feeling someone was watching her.

She knew about the crazies who stalked celebrities. A

friend had suffered that kind of unwanted attention from a fan without a life. The experience, even viewed from the outside, was spooky and frightening.

This was different.

The first time, she'd been on the cliff posing for Maurice with her back to the sea. Suddenly a door in the castle opened and a man stepped into the garden.

Nothing unusual in that. A place like this would employ a gardener. Half a dozen of them, for all she knew.

He'd walked slowly to the low wall that surrounded the garden, tucked his hands into his pockets and just stood there. Watching her. Or maybe watching the mechanics of the shoot. That was what she'd told herself, when he'd remained motionless for the next five or six minutes. People always gathered to watch when you did a shoot on a street corner or at a resort.

Later the same afternoon, the *Bridal Dreams* bunch had all been down on the beach, Maurice photographing her in the bridal gown, some moody shot he'd print in blacks and grays, with her standing so that the lacy hem of the gown trailed in the water. She'd been posing, smiling, pouting, whatever felt right or whatever Maurice demanded…

And she'd felt it again. Eyes, watching her.

A figure stood on the cliff. A man. Tall, broad-shouldered, narrow-hipped, standing with his legs slightly apart, his arms folded across his chest and the wind blowing his dark hair back from his face. The distance was too great for her to make out his features.

The sight of him was intriguing. That hard-looking body. The jeans that fit him like a glove, the black T-shirt, black-lensed sunglasses.

Who was he? Why did the sight of him make her breath catch?

She knew he was watching her, just as she knew he wasn't a crazy, some guy who'd fallen in love with her photo and wanted to tell her that they came from neighboring galaxies. She knew it in the most scientific way possible.

Her instincts told her so.

Fallon rolled her eyes, just thinking it, and Maurice's voice pulled her into the present.

"I don't want smirks, I want pensive," he shouted.

She nodded, took some deep breaths and gave him pensive.

The man always stayed at a distance, watching her as if he wanted to absorb her into his skin. At the same time he wanted to turn his back and forget he'd ever seen her.

Another scientific deduction. Besides, even if it was true, it made no sense.

The evidence all pointed to his watching not her but the entire group. He was surely one of the security guards that patrolled the place, and if she hadn't noticed him right away, that was just because he was good at blending into the scenery.

And if her sun-baked brain gave him more depth than that, painted him as almost cruelly masculine and incredibly sexy, that was her fault, not his.

Fallon blew the hair back from her forehead. Without question, the heat was playing games with her mind.

"Maurice?" She swung toward the photographer, hands on her hips. "Listen, Maurice, enough is enough. I'm melting. My makeup's running, my scalp's crawling with sweat."

"You want me to tell you you still look gorgeous? 'Cause you do."

"Yeah, right. That's wonderful, but I've had it."

"Ten minutes more, that's all. Lift your chin like so."

"You said ten minutes an hour ago."

Maurice lifted his chin. Fallon left hers where it was.

"Maurice," she said firmly, "everybody else has gone. They're all sitting in the tent, out of the sun, drinking something cold and waiting for you so they can take the van back to the inn."

"Let them wait. I'm not finished. Look at me, O'Connell. Give me a little more attitude. You're a bride and your groom's watching you and you want to show him what you've got. Good. Fine.''

Did she want to show the man who watched her what she had? She'd thought about him last night, lying in her narrow, lumpy bed. Imagined his face. Would his eyes be dark? His nose classically Roman? His mouth full, his jaw chiseled?

Would he look like the man at the airport?

The skin on the back of Fallon's neck tingled. He was up there, watching her again.

She knew it.

She looked back, shading her eyes, making no attempt to be discreet and yes, there he was, standing with his arms folded, his eyes hidden behind those omnipresent dark glasses.

A hot arrow of desire shot through her so quickly, so unexpectedly, that she felt her knees turn to water. She wanted—she wanted—

Out of here. That was what she wanted. Turning, she splashed through the shallows to the beach.

"O'Connell?"

Her sunglasses were on a canvas folding chair. She jabbed them on her nose and shoved her feet into a pair of rubber thongs.

"What's happening, babe?"

"The session's over, that's what's happening."

"Yeah, but the light's changing." Maurice hurried after her as she headed for the path that wound up the cliff. "Babe," he whined, "look at the sky. Clouds, see? And the water's getting choppy. Nice little waves coming in. Moody stuff. I thought we'd try something new—"

"I'll see you later," Fallon said, and started up the path. Maurice was a great photographer but he never knew when to stop.

She did, and it was now.

She was out of breath by the time she reached level ground. The stranger was gone, which annoyed her. What kind of man watched a woman without making an effort to meet her? Because yes, he was watching her. Not the others.

Her.

Fallon strode toward the tent, where the *Bridal Dreams* people were sprawled in a semi-circular arrangement of canvas chairs, their faces tilted up to the sun.

Andy looked up and called out to her. "All done?"

She nodded. He grinned and gave her a thumbs-up. She grinned back, returned the gesture and opened the door of the ancient little red Fiat she'd rented from the innkeeper as soon as she'd realized how isolated this place was.

Her jeans and T-shirt were lying in the back seat. Fallon pulled them on over her bikini, grimacing a little at the feel of the hot cotton against her sticky skin.

She wanted a shower and a cold drink. She wanted to pack her things for tomorrow's flight home and then, maybe, drive up into the hills for one last look over the sea.

Most of all, she thought as she let out the clutch and floored the gas pedal, most of all, she never wanted to see this cliff and its *castello* again.

Stefano watched Fallon O'Connell walk toward the tent he'd permitted to be raised on his property.

She seemed to be in a hurry to leave.

Was he the reason? Yes. He probably was.

Stefano opened the concealed minifridge built into the wall behind his desk, took out a bottle of water and raised it to his lips.

The lady thought he was watching her. He'd realized that days ago. The way she stiffened and looked around her whenever he appeared was a dead giveaway.

It didn't surprise him. Women who looked like her assumed they had the eye of every man who saw them.

She was wrong. He wanted nothing to do with her.

Concern for his privacy had drawn him back, not a woman, and a damned good thing, too. Carla had violated their agreement before he'd even had time to board his plane. She'd brought in more people than she'd said she would, and his housekeeper told him that she'd sought access to the house the instant his back was turned.

Stefano settled into a leather armchair, put his feet up on a hassock and took another drink of cold water.

Of course, he'd sent Carla packing. He'd wanted to toss out the lot of them, her and her hedonistic *fashionistas*, too, but that dark threat she'd made hung over his head. Instead, he'd done the best he could, told his former mistress to get off his property before he had her thrown off.

Then he'd settled in to get through the week without going crazy from boredom, and that was the only reason he'd taken to observing the *Bridal Dreams* group.

Fallon had reached the disreputable-looking old car she'd picked up somewhere. Stefano frowned as she opened the door, pulled out jeans and a T-shirt and slipped them on. The shirt was oversize but the jeans clung to her legs. Such impossibly long legs, he thought with lazy appraisal.

Clothed, she was as magnificent as she'd been in the string bikini.

Okay. Maybe he paid more attention to her than to the others. What man wouldn't? She was stunning, the kind of woman who'd silence a room simply by entering it. A man would have to be blind not to enjoy looking at her.

Tomorrow, there'd be nothing to look at.

This unwanted intrusion in his life was over. This was the last day the photographic crew would be here. Fallon O'Connell was driving away right now. He couldn't help smiling at the way the little Fiat bucked. She'd probably let the clutch out too fast. She was driving too fast, too, leaving a plume of dust behind.

The photographer had joined the others near the tent.

Soon, they'd climb into their hired van and then—and then, he'd never see Fallon again.

Stefano got to his feet and paced to the window.

He'd never see any of these people again. That was what he'd meant.

The Fiat disappeared in the grove of trees that led to the gate. The van followed scant seconds later. Stefano raised the half-empty water bottle in mock salute.

Good riddance to the lot of them.

His world was his own again. No more unwanted voices, drifting from the beach. No more people tromping across the ruins or standing on the edge of the cliff, looking out at his sea and his volcano.

No more Fallon O'Connell, with that lush mouth he'd dreamed of tasting, those high breasts that surely would fill his senses with their perfumed heat, those incredible legs that he could imagine wrapped around his hips.

Stefano frowned and put down the bottle.

All right. So his disinterest was a lie. The truth was that he'd watched her like a damned hawk, felt his body turn hard for her, pretended he hadn't wanted to take her to bed when it was all he'd wanted from the second she scrambled into his car. He'd watched her pose for the camera, seen her feign expressions of excitement and lust, and known he could make her actually feel those things, make her eyes long for the sight of him, her soft voice cry out for him, for his possession…

Was he losing his mind?

Stefano strode out of his study, through the kitchen where his housekeeper looked up in surprise.

"Signore? Avete desiderato qualcosa?"

"No," he said, trying to sound polite, knowing he sounded anything but that. "Thank you, Anna. I don't want anything. *Grazie.* I'm going out riding. Don't bother making me supper."

Anna pursed her lips. She was a small, thin woman, Sicilian to the marrow of her bones, and the only thing she seemed to want more than to fatten him up was to turn him into a true *Siciliano* who could read everything in the rise and fall of insect voices or the wind blowing in from the sea.

"A storm is coming. There will be wind and rain."

"I'll be fine."

"In the dark, the roads will be treacherous."

Just what he needed. A second Italian grandmother.

"I'll probably be back long before then."

Anna gave a deep sigh. "As you wish, *Padrone*."

As he wished? Stefano almost laughed as he went into the garage and shut the door behind him. He walked past the first three bays to the last, stroked a hand lightly over the gleaming black Harley that was his vehicle of choice wherever the roads were narrow and twisting.

If things were as he wished, Fallon O'Connell would either be waiting in his bed or he wouldn't be thinking about her at all.

He put on his helmet and his black leather jacket, pressed the button and waited while the door slid up. Then he straddled the bike and kick-started it to roaring life.

He knew where she was staying, knew he could go there and confront her, tell her that the hot flash of sexual awareness he'd seen in her eyes when they met pulsed within him, too.

But he wouldn't.

Wanting her was a weakness. She was a friend of Carla's, a citizen of Carla's gaudy world. Besides, wanting any woman was a weakness just now. Carla had left a bad taste in his mouth. Didn't people say that celibacy—temporary celibacy—was good for the soul?

God knew his soul could use all the help it could get.

Stefano snapped down the visor of his helmet and roared out of the garage. A long, hard ride would calm him down.

So would the knowledge that he would never lay eyes on Fallon O'Connell again.

An hour later, the island was wrapped in the black, wet, howling embrace of the storm Anna had predicted.

The wind was a wild thing, tearing at Stefano as he came around a tight curve on a narrow road. Another mile, maybe two, and he'd be—

What in hell was that?

The bright beam of his headlight pierced the darkness and picked out the shape of a small car coming toward him.

"Sweet Jesus," Stefano said, and braked, but it was too late. The driver of the car must have seen him, too, and braked as he had, but too hard. The car skidded and swerved across his path and he knew, with terrifying clarity, that it was heading directly for a gnarled tree, but it was the rest of what he saw in that sudden blaze of light that tore a cry from his throat.

The car was an old red Fiat. And the horrified face of the woman behind the wheel, her mouth drawn open in a scream Stefano could not hear, was Fallon's.

CHAPTER FOUR

TIRES squealed agonizingly as they fought for purchase on the wet road, but nothing could stop the forward momentum of the Fiat as it slid, with sickening inevitability, into the tree.

Stefano leaped off his motorcycle and ran toward the car.

"Fallon," he shouted, "Fallon!"

The night was silent except for the incessant drumming of the rain and the pounding of his own pulse.

His first thought was that she was okay. She'd managed to slow her speed considerably before the crash and the damage to the car seemed confined to a crumpled fender.

When he reached the car, he groaned aloud.

It was an old car, with no airbag to have cushioned Fallon from the force of the crash. The windshield on the driver's side was shattered. She lay slumped against the steering wheel, and tiny shards of glass glittered like stars in her dark hair.

Stefano grabbed the handle. The door wouldn't give.

"Come on," he shouted, "come on, damn it!"

Desperate, his breath sobbing in his throat, he pulled harder. It was useless. The door was either locked or jammed shut.

He cursed, ran around the car, slipping and sliding in the wet dirt, wrenched open the passenger door and climbed inside.

"Fallon?" he said as he reached for her.

She didn't respond.

Tearing off one glove, he slid his fingers to her wrist. Yes, thank God, he could feel the beat of her pulse.

She was alive.

His belly knotted when he saw that she hadn't fastened her seat belt. If only she'd worn the belt. If only it hadn't been raining. If only he hadn't come around the curve just then.

Stefano blanked all those "if onlys" from his head. All that mattered was what he did next. The accident, everything that led up to it, was part of the past and couldn't be changed.

He started to move her, then froze as his mind played back everything he'd ever read or heard about the folly of moving someone who'd been in a bad accident.

You could make a bad injury worse, cause paralysis or death.

Did those caveats apply when you were on a road in the middle of nowhere with the rain pouring down? He knew these roads and these mountains. The odds of someone coming along to offer help ranged from zero to none. There was a farmhouse perhaps ten miles away. With luck, it would have a telephone.

For the first time in his life, Stefano was immobilized by indecision. Should he move Fallon? Ride his bike to the farmhouse, hope there was a phone, call for an ambulance, then come back to be with her?

Gritting his teeth, praying to whatever deity might be listening, Stefano eased Fallon into his arms, then drew her carefully toward him. She moaned once but made no other sound.

He paused when he got her into the passenger seat. Holding her in the crook of first one arm and then the other, he shrugged free of his heavy leather jacket and wrapped it around her. Her head was still down but her breathing was steady.

"I've got you now, sweetheart," he whispered. "You're safe."

Still, no response.

Holding her to him, gently, his hands trembling, he tipped her head up.

Oh, God!

Her face. Her beautiful face!

Crimson streamed from a gash on her forehead that reached into her hairline, from another on her cheek, from yet a third that slashed wickedly across her chin. She had no other wounds that he could see, but those were enough. Knowing who she was, what she was, Stefano understood that what had happened on this night would forever change Fallon O'Connell's life.

His heart lurched.

"Fallon," he said softly, "can you hear me?"

She moaned again. Her lashes fluttered.

He leaned closer. "Fallon?"

Her eyes opened and she stared blindly at him.

"What—what happened?" she said in a weak voice.

"There's been an accident."

"An accident?"

"Yes." He searched for words that would reassure her. "You're going to be all right."

"I don't—I don't remember…"

"That's all right. You don't have to remember. Not just yet. Fallon?"

"Mmm?"

She was tumbling back into unconsciousness. Was it best to let that happen or to keep her awake? Damn it, why didn't he know? He'd sat through a first-aid course in college. Had he been asleep?

Stefano turned his face to the sky, let the rain beat down on him.

What did you do for someone who'd suffered head trauma?

"Fallon. Listen to me."

"I'm lis'ning."

"Tell me where you hurt."

"Sleepy."

"Yes. I know, but first tell me if you hurt anywhere. Your arms? Your legs?" He took a deep breath. "Your back?"

"Head," she whispered, and punctuated the word with a hiss of pain. "Head hurts."

She lifted her hand and raised it to her forehead. Stefano caught her wrist, afraid she might do more damage to her wounds and even more afraid the awful reality of what had happened might send her into shock.

"Listen to me, Fallon. I have to get help."

"Don'leave me."

He wound his fingers through hers. "Only for a little while," he said softly.

No reply. Her lashes drifted to her cheeks but, God, she wasn't sleeping. Not with her face so pale, her blood so dark.

Stefano lifted her hand to his lips and pressed his mouth to her knuckles. Then he got to his feet, wincing at the sudden pain that shot through his arm.

Pain in his arm? Was he hurt? He looked down at his forearm, saw an ugly gash oozing blood. He must have cut himself on something, glass from the windshield or torn metal on the car. Whatever had happened, it meant he probably wouldn't be able to carry her very far.

Not that carrying her to shelter was a real option. The rain was coming down so hard he half expected Noah and the ark to come floating by.

Okay. Maybe he didn't remember much about how to treat an accident victim, but it certainly didn't make sense to expose a woman who might be going into shock to the force of a cold rainstorm.

What then? Leave her here, alone? No. That was out of the question.

He looked at the Fiat. A crushed fender and a smashed windshield didn't necessarily preclude the engine from working.

There was only one way to find out.

Hands shaking, he fastened the seat belt around Fallon. Then he climbed over her, brushed glass off the driver's seat and got behind the wheel. Carefully, holding his breath, he turned the key.

The starter motor whined. The engine coughed once, twice. Then, with a shudder and the squeal of metal on metal, it started. It didn't sound as if it would last very long but all he needed was to coax ten miles or so out of it, if luck was with him.

He got the car into gear and backed it away from the tree, shifted gears again, made a tight, cautious U-turn and stopped.

The wound on his arm was throbbing; he could feel a cold sweat break out on his forehead and his teeth were starting to chatter. Shock, he figured, and only gave a damn because it might mean he had less time to get help for Fallon than he'd thought.

He looked at her.

She sat with her head lolling against the headrest, her face still pale, the blood starting to coagulate. Her battered flesh was starting to swell. Such perfection, so cruelly destroyed.

His throat constricted and he leaned closer and feathered his lips over hers.

Then he took a deep breath, put the car in gear again and began what he suspected might be the most important journey of his life.

Pain. Pain, sharp and throbbing. Harsh white light. A smell of something coldly antiseptic.

And voices. A woman's, brisk and demanding, speaking in Italian, followed by a man's, urgent and low-pitched, speaking American English.

"Signorina O'Connell. *Apra I vostri occhi.*"

"Fallon? Come on. Open your eyes."

Open her eyes? Could she do that? She wanted to; it

was awful to lie here this way, trapped in the dark. Was she asleep and dreaming? If she fought hard enough, could she compel her eyes to open?

"Fallon. Please. Look at me."

Sorry, she thought. *Sorry, but I can't.*

Her eyelids were weighted down.

Down, down, down.

Fallon tumbled back into darkness.

"Fallon."

Fallon sighed. It was that husky male voice again, calling her back.

"I know you can hear me, Fallon. I want you to open your eyes."

He was half-right, whoever he was. She could hear him, but opening her eyes was impossible.

"You can do it."

A hand, hard and warm, wrapped around hers.

"I know you can do it."

He was wrong. She couldn't do anything but lie here and sleep.

"Damn it, don't you want to get better? You won't, if you don't open your eyes. You have to wake up. You must wake up!"

"*Signore.* I know you're upset but please, you need some rest. *Il dottore* would like to check your arm again. I know you refused stitches earlier, but if you would just come with me—"

"Not until she's conscious."

"*Si,* so you said, but that might take hours." The woman's voice gentled. "Days, perhaps, *signore.*"

"Then I'll stay with her for days," the man said roughly. "I'll stay as long as it takes."

"You need to take care of your own injury, *signore.*"

"You need to take care of your own injury," Fallon said weakly, as she opened her eyes. "She's right."

The man and the woman swung toward her, staring at her as if they couldn't believe she'd spoken.

Well, why would they? She'd thought the words, but they hadn't come out sounding quite like that. Her speech was stiff and slurred.

That didn't seem to matter to the people standing beside her bed. Both of them said her name with excitement.

"Signorina O'Connell!"

"Fallon! Fallon, thank God."

Fallon looked from one face to the other. The woman was dressed in white and was obviously a nurse. The man—the man looked familiar. Dark hair. Dark eyes. A smile that softened an otherwise hard-looking mouth.

Who was he? Why couldn't she recall his name? It lay just at the tip of her tongue.

"It's good to have you with us again, *signorina*," the nurse said. "How do you feel?"

It was a good question. How *did* she feel? Exhausted. Achy all over. Confused. But most of all, her head hurt. And her face. From the neck up, she was a throbbing mass of pain.

"Whappen?"

"*Scusi?*"

"She wants to know what happened."

The man reached for her hand and laced his fingers through hers. It felt good, letting him do that. He was strong; she could tell by just looking into his eyes, and with their fingers entwined, she could almost feel some of that strength flowing into her.

"There was an accident," he said softly.

"Accident?"

"Yes. A car accident."

A car accident? Fallon closed her eyes, tried to remember. She saw herself in a car, saw a winding, wet road, a bright light, a tree...

And then nothing.

"Fallon?"

She made the mistake of shaking her head to tell him she had no memory of it. Tiny hammer-blows of pain struck along her jaw, her forehead, scalp and eye socket. She hissed with the sharpness of it.

That sent the nurse into action.

"I shall get *il dottore,*" she said, and hurried away.

A bell was ringing softly in the background; a mechanical-sounding voice was repeating a message over and over, requesting that a *Dottore* Something-or-other call his office.

Fallon looked into the man's eyes.

"Is this a hospital?"

The words didn't come out sounding like that. *Izissaspital?* was closer to what she said, but evidently he understood because he nodded.

"Yes."

A hospital. Of course. What other place would be so dazzlingly bright? The walls, the ceiling; even the unadorned light fixture in the ceiling blazed down with a white glow so vivid it hurt the eyes.

"The doctor will be here in a moment."

The nurse was back, politely trying to get past the man, but he didn't give an inch.

"*Signore, par favore,* if you would let go of the lady's hand for a moment... I promise, I'll give it right back."

Color stained his high cheekbones. He let go of Fallon's hand and she felt a flutter of alarm. He was the only familiar thing—the only vaguely familiar thing—in this strange and painful world.

"Don'go," she whispered.

His expression softened. "Don't worry, *cara.* I won't leave you."

The nurse's cool fingers closed around her wrist.

"Her pulse is okay?" the man said.

"Fine."

"Her temperature? It's okay, too?"

"I'll know after I take it," the nurse said gently. "Just

be patient, *signore.*'' A moment passed. The nurse nodded, put a stethoscope to her ears, listened and nodded again. ''The *signorina's* vital signs are excellent. I'll go and inform the doctor.''

She stood up; the man brushed past her and sat down beside the bed. When he touched Fallon's hand, she twined her fingers through his.

''What can I do for her?'' he asked the nurse in a low voice.

''You have already done a great deal,'' the woman said quietly. ''Getting her here as quickly as you did...''

''Yes.'' His eyes went dark. ''I meant the rest.''

''You can be here, *signore.*'' She smiled at Fallon. ''That seems to mean a great deal to the lady, *si?*''

It did. He was her only comfort...and yet—and yet—Why did he seem familiar? Why couldn't she place him?

''I don't remember you,'' Fallon said woozily. ''But I have the feeling that I should.''

''The gentleman brought you here,'' the nurse said, before Stefano could speak. ''He is, how do you say, your Good Samaritan, yes?''

Fallon knew better than to nod her head this time. She knew better than to smile, either. Moving her mouth was too painful.

''Yes,'' she said softly, and looked at Stefano. ''Did you find me on the road?''

''Not exactly.''

His hand tightened on hers as the nurse padded quietly from the room. Stefano chewed on his lip. Nothing about this little scene was simple. Should he tell Fallon she was right to find his face familiar? Should he remind her of their initial meeting and how badly it had gone? Should he tell her he'd been watching her all week?

No. She was shaken and hurt, and things would get far worse before they got better, for she had yet to see her face in a mirror and realize the severity of her injuries.

But he could tell her what had happened on that wet road.

"You were driving your car," he said in a low voice. "I was riding my motorcycle. The road was narrow, the rain had just started and you came around a curve and skidded." He hesitated. "You didn't expect to see anyone else on that road and when you did—"

"Were you hurt, too?"

"Me? No. I'm fine." He cleared his throat. "Would you like some water?"

She nodded. He took a glass from the table beside the bed and carefully brought it to her lips. She tried to sit up, but he wouldn't let her.

"No, no. Don't move around. Not until the doctor checks you over. Here." He slid his arm around her shoulders, lifted her a bit and gently tucked the straw between her lips. "Drink a little. Easy. That's it. Good?"

Fallon nodded again and sank back against the pillows.

"How do you feel?"

"Awful," she said, and tried to smile but it didn't work. For one thing, it hurt. And the muscles in her face wouldn't cooperate. She lifted her hand, raised it toward her face. The man caught her wrist and stopped her.

"You have bandages," he said quickly. "It's probably best if you don't touch them."

"Bandages?"

"Yes. It'll be all right. You'll see."

"Bandages on my face? Am I cut?"

He could hear the underlying note of fear in her voice and knew he would have willingly done anything to take that fear away. How much to tell her? How soon?

"A little," he finally said.

Her eyes searched his. He saw the muscles in her throat move as she swallowed and he knew she had decided not to ask too many questions just yet.

God, he wanted to take her in his arms, hold her, soothe her as if she were a little girl needing his comfort.

"Tell me more about the accident."

"There's nothing more to tell," he said, clasping her hand again. "What matters is that you're alive and that you'll be walking out of here in no time."

Then, why wouldn't her Good Samaritan let her touch her face? Before he could stop her, Fallon snaked her other hand out from under the blanket and lifted. Her fingers danced over the bandages, then felt the puckered ridgelines of delicate silk stitches.

She felt her stomach tighten, then drop.

"More than bandages," she started to say in a shaky whisper, but just then the door opened and the nurse and a plump man in a white coat entered the room.

"Ah, *Signorina* O'Connell," he said in barely accented English, "how good to see you awake. I am Dr. Scalfani. How do you feel? Never mind. Not so good, I am sure, but we will make you feel much better, very soon. *Signore?* If you would wait in the hall…"

The man rose to his feet. "I'll be right outside," he said, leaning toward her and smiling. "Okay?"

Fallon gave his hand a last squeeze. "Tell me your name," she whispered.

"My name is Stefano. Stefano Lucchesi," Stefano said, and waited for her reaction, just as he'd waited for a reaction when she first opened her eyes and saw him.

There was none. Why would she recall his face, when she'd only met him the one time? Why would she recall his name, just because he'd introduced himself to her that day? He hadn't forgotten anything about her, but that didn't mean she'd had the same response to him.

"*Signore?*"

Stefano nodded. "Yes. Sorry. I'll wait outside."

The doctor poked and prodded, hummed to himself and spoke in rapid snatches of Italian to the nurse. Finally, he touched Fallon's face.

"I apologize," he said, "but I will be quick."

It hurt. Oh, it hurt, it hurt, it hurt.

"I know, *signorina*," he said quietly. "You are in pain, yes?"

"My face…" She licked her lips, trying to find the right words yet afraid to say them. "Is there a lot of damage to my face?"

The doctor's gaze softened. "I don't know," he said bluntly. "It's too soon to tell what will heal and what will scar. I wish I could give you a more complete answer, but I can't."

Fallon looked past him, her eyes fixed on the empty white wall.

"I'm a model," she said in a low voice. "My face…"

"Yes. I understand. But being alive is the important thing, *signorina*. If not for the gentleman who brought you here, who knows what might have happened?"

Fallon nodded, even though it hurt.

"Yes," she said calmly, "who knows what might have happened?"

Without any warning, she began to weep.

The doctor patted her shoulder and murmured to the nurse. Fallon felt something warm slide through her veins.

Just before she sank into blackness, Stefano Lucchesi sat down on the chair beside her and reached for her hand. In a dizzying flash of light, she turned her gaze on him.

"I remember you," she said clearly, and then she fell into the darkness.

Another day slipped by. Fallon awakened, slept, awakened again.

And she was better.

Things hurt less; she wasn't groggy. The doctor examined her, hummed with pleasure and said she was on the road to recovery.

This time, she fell into a true sleep. When she awoke, the room was filled with daylight.

"Fallon. Welcome back. How do you feel?"

She turned her head and saw Stefano Lucchesi. Oh, yes.

She remembered him. He was as good-looking as the first time they'd met except now he looked exhausted; there was a heavy black stubble on his jaw and though she suspected he'd been beside her all the time, all she could think about was how he had mocked her for making her living as a model.

"What are you doing here?"

"I told you I'd stay with you, didn't I?"

"I don't want you with me, *signore.*"

His smile tilted. Until this moment, he hadn't been sure if what she'd said meant she really did remember him.

He knew the answer now.

"You recalled our first meeting," he said flatly.

"Yes." Fallon took a deep breath. "So, our paths have crossed twice, Signore Lucchesi."

"More than that," Stefano said. Why not get it out in the open? "You spent the week being photographed at my castle."

"At your…" She stared at him. "No wonder you knew exactly where I was going the day you told me how ridiculous it was that people should pay money to photograph me."

"I never said that."

"Incredible. First you insulted me, then you gave me a choice between crashing into a tree or killing you."

"That's not what happened."

He was right. She still couldn't recall the entire accident, but enough bits and pieces had come back so she knew it hadn't been his fault. Still, he deserved to feel guilty. The way he'd disparaged her occupation, and now this…

She knew it was wrong to put the two together, but it was almost as if fate had listened to his put-down of her and stepped in to lend a hand.

Why should she be the only one in pain?

"Your breakfast is here. Would you like to eat it?"

His voice was stiff but she had to give him credit; he

hadn't marched out the door. He might not feel guilty about the accident but he felt guilty about something, she thought grimly, and tried not to imagine how alone she'd have been if he'd left.

She looked at the tray table. Two white plastic drink containers and a small plastic cup stood on it.

"Juice," Stefano said. "Coffee, and what looks like cherry Jell-O. What would you like?"

"Nothing."

"You have to eat to get well."

"You should have told me you owned that castle."

"Yes, I should have. Does that make you feel better? Are we keeping score here? One for O'Connell, nothing for Lucchesi. Now stop being a fool and sit up and have some of this slop."

Fallon laughed. Not a good idea, considering that it hurt her entire face, but how could she not laugh at what he'd said?

And, if she wanted to be honest, how could she not admit that he'd scored points, too? If it weren't for Stefano Lucchesi, who knew how long it would have been before someone found her and brought her to the hospital?

"Maybe—maybe I'll try the coffee," she said after a few seconds. "If you'd ring for the nurse to lift the bed—"

Instead, he put his arm around her, eased her up against the pillows and brought the coffee to her lips.

"Easy. Don't drink too fast. How's that?"

"Awful," she said, but she sucked down half the contents of the container before falling back against the pillows.

"Thank you." There was no reason she couldn't be polite.

"You're welcome."

The silence stretched between them uncomfortably until Fallon cleared her throat.

"How long?"

"Since the accident? Two days."

"Two days." She moistened her lips. "Well, Mr. Lucchesi—"

"Stefano."

"It was—generous of you to spend so much time here, but I'm all right now, so—"

"You're going to be fine."

"Sure."

"I know things look bleak right now, but everything will work out." Stefano took her hand. "I swear it."

He spoke quietly and with such conviction that she turned her head and looked at him, wondering if she'd ever seen a stronger face, a more determined jaw.

She took a deep breath.

"I want to see my face," she said softly.

He blanched. "I don't think—"

"Please."

It was the "please," said in a shaky whisper, that did it. There was a mirror on the dresser. The nurse had pointed it out to him. "If the *signorina* should ask," she'd said, and he'd told himself that if Fallon did ask, he hoped he was a hundred miles away.

Stefano got the mirror and brought it to her. Her breasts rose and fell beneath the plain white hospital gown as she took a deep breath, and then she lifted the mirror and looked into it.

Stefano waited. Would she weep? Curse? For all he knew, she might faint. What hadn't been covered with bandages was now a canvas of black and purple and angry red.

Fallon didn't do anything he'd expected. Instead, she stared at herself while time dragged by, the only sign of what she was feeling visible in the tremor of the mirror, which finally fell from her hand to the bed.

She lay her head back and shut her eyes. Tears seeped from beneath the shelter of her lashes and tracked down her face like tiny diamonds.

It was Stefano who mouthed an obscenity as he reached to comfort her. She slapped away his hands and turned her face to the side.

"Go away."

"Fallon—"

"Are you deaf? I told you to get out."

"So you can wallow in self-pity?"

Her eyes flew open as she turned toward him. It had been a low blow and he knew it. She'd been brave and strong and he supposed she'd earned the right to some self-pity, if that was what she wanted, but he also knew that sympathy wasn't going to give her the courage to face whatever might come next, the weeks, maybe months, of healing; the decisions about possible further surgery and, most of all, the changes all this would bring to her life.

"Who the hell do you think you are?" she said, her voice quavering with anger. "You have no right—"

"The Chinese say that if you save a person's life, you become responsible for that person."

Her eyes flashed. "Then I guess we're both lucky that neither of us is Chinese."

"You survived a bad accident. Are you going to give up now?"

"That's my business."

"You're wrong. It's my business, too." He clasped her hands tightly in his. "There's some truth to what you said. You might not have had that accident if you hadn't come around that curve and seen me."

"Ah. Now I understand. You feel guilty. Well, don't. What happened was nobody's fault but mine. Okay? Now will you get the hell out of this room and leave me—"

Stefano silenced the bitter words by leaning over and brushing his lips over hers. She gave a soft gasp of surprise and he thought how sweet the whisper of her breath was before he drew back.

"I'm not leaving," he said in a low voice. "You might as well accept that."

Fallon stared at him. Of course he was leaving. She didn't want him here, didn't want anyone to see her like this, to be kind to her or gentle because if they were, she knew she'd break down, sob out all the terror and anguish in her heart...

But he was still there when she awakened hours later, and the next day, when she took her first steps, it was his arm she leaned on for support.

He was there until the day she was discharged and she told herself she wasn't looking for him all that morning, that she wasn't straining to hear the sound of his voice as she made phone calls, arranged for a taxi, for a hotel room in Catania where she would stay until she felt strong enough to face not just the long flight home but the shock and sympathy of her mother, her stepfather, her brothers and sisters and everyone who would have to see what she saw each time she looked in the mirror.

At her request, an aide bought her dark glasses and a wide-brimmed hat. Fallon put them on just before she stepped out the front door of the hospital for the first time in five days.

Oh, how blue the sky, how soft the air. She put back her head, drew a deep, deep breath.

"Fallon."

Startled, she looked toward the curb. A black Mercedes had pulled alongside it. Stefano was framed in the open door. He smiled, stepped from the car and came toward her.

"Stefano," she said, and when he held out his arms, she went straight into them.

CHAPTER FIVE

FALLON sat curled in a window seat at *Castello Lucchesi,* her arms wrapped around her drawn-up knees as she stared out over the sea.

She had been in Stefano's home for three days and she'd spent all of that time here, in one of the castle's guest suites.

A taut smile angled across her mouth as she thought back to that day more than two weeks ago when she'd come to Sicily anticipating the luxury of being housed in a castle, in a suite just like this, only to have Carla tell her that plans had changed.

"The owner is an unpleasant old man," she'd said. "He won't permit us inside his house."

Fallon sighed and lay her cheek against her raised knees.

Wrong on all counts. The castle's owner was gracious, even generous. He'd not only let her inside his home, he'd insisted she stay in it. He was young, surely no more than in his mid-thirties, vital, and so ruggedly handsome that any normal woman would surely feel her pulse quicken whenever she saw him.

But Fallon wasn't a normal woman anymore. She was a patchwork creature of bruises, stitches and swellings, and it would be a very long time before she'd react to a man again, or maybe it was closer to the truth that it would be a long time before a man reacted to her.

What man would want to touch a woman who looked the way she did?

Stefano had held her, even kissed her, but he'd been offering comfort. And, God, she was grateful for those soft touches, that light pressure of his lips against hers. He'd made her feel less alone, less grotesque.

Except, she wasn't going to take advantage of his kindness.

He'd brought her to her rooms that first day.

Fallon felt her face heat.

Brought her? He'd carried her, first up the wide stone steps outside the castle, then up the impressive stairwell that wound from the great entrance hall to the second floor.

"I can walk," she'd insisted, but her protest had only made him hold her more closely.

She'd heard the steady beat of his heart beneath her ear, felt the warmth of his body, and something had stirred deep inside her, an emotion as unwelcome in her new life as a hot flow of lava would be to this island.

She couldn't even think about herself as a sexual creature. Who would gaze into her battered face and want her? It was only that being in his arms felt so safe.

She had never felt as safe before.

When he'd shouldered open the door to the guest suite and sat her gently on the edge of a massive four-poster bed, she'd wanted to beg him not to let go of her. Instead, she'd drawn free of his arms.

"Thank you," she'd said politely. "You're being very kind."

"My motives aren't all that altruistic," he'd replied, and smiled. "*Castello Lucchesi* is brand-new. A new house needs a guest for luck. It's an old Sicilian saying."

"You're American," Fallon said, smiling a little in return. "And you just made that up."

Stefano grinned. "Maybe. But wait until you see the lunch Anna—my housekeeper—prepared. She's all excited about having someone besides me to cook for."

"Lunch?"

What would it be like to eat in a dining room instead of a hospital room, to have Stefano look at her across an expanse of linen and china? It had been simpler in the hospital. Dressed in a shapeless gown, perched on the edge of a narrow bed, she'd been a patient and he'd been a visitor. Now she was his guest, and the contrast between her battered face and the elegance of his home would be stark.

"Yes," he said, still smiling. "At one. You can sit outside afterward—there's a patio that looks onto the garden. Or I'll bring you back upstairs so you can take a nap, if you're tired. Dinner isn't until—"

"I really don't feel up to coming downstairs just yet," she said quickly. "Would your housekeeper mind bringing me my meals on a tray?"

"I should have thought of that. Tell you what. I'll ask her to set a table on the balcony just off your bedroom, and I'll join you here for meals until you feel up to—"

"No," she'd said quickly. "I mean, thank you, that's a kind offer, but I really don't feel up to company. You understand."

"Of course." He'd cleared his throat. "You're probably exhausted."

"I'm a little tired, yes."

"Tomorrow, then."

"Why don't I—why don't I ask… Anna? Is that right? Why don't I ask Anna to let you know when I'm feeling better."

His eyes had darkened in that way she knew meant he was displeased, but he'd said yes, certainly, he'd do as she preferred. Now two days had gone by and, true to his word, Stefano had left her alone.

Fallon sighed and sat up straight in the window seat.

The truth was, she was going crazy up here. The suite was handsome and spacious; there were magazines and books carefully arranged on a table in the sitting room and there was a TV set with satellite reception in the bedroom, but she didn't want to read or watch TV, she wanted to walk on the cliffs, explore the ruins, run on the beach.

Most of all, she wanted to see Stefano.

But she couldn't. Not when he didn't want to see her. If he did, he'd have come up here, knocked on the door and insisted she stop being a recluse.

Yes, she'd told him that was what she wanted, but she'd lied. Couldn't he figure that out? Didn't he *want* to figure it out? Was he just as happy she'd chosen solitude so that he didn't have to look at her, and wasn't that kind of paranoid thinking absolutely crazy?

The throaty growl of an engine below the window caught her attention. Fallon looked out just as a shiny black motorcycle and its rider wheeled into view from what she assumed was the garage. The rider stopped the bike to put on his helmet and, as he did, he looked up.

It was Stefano.

His eyes met hers. No smile. No wave. Just those dark eyes, burning into hers, and then his mouth twisted, he slammed down the visor, bent low over the bike and roared away.

Oh, God!

He'd seen her face for the first time in a couple of days, and she'd seen his reaction to it. As kind as he'd been, he hadn't been able to keep the truth from showing. It was how everyone would look at her from now on, with mingled expressions of pity and disgust and—

Fallon shot to her feet.

And, she really was going to go insane if she didn't get out of this silk-walled prison. She needed to leave this place and go where nobody knew her. It was what she should have done right away.

It took a while to figure out how to phone for a taxi but after a frustrating few minutes, she finally made the necessary arrangements. How long would Stefano be gone? She had no way of knowing; she only knew she had to be out of here before he returned.

The inn had sent over her luggage; Anna had put her things neatly into the closet. Now, hands shaking, Fallon tossed her suitcase on the bed, tore her clothing from the racks and shelves and dumped it inside. She was wearing a light cotton summer dress and sandals; they'd do for her taxi ride to a hotel. Any hotel. She'd ask the driver for a recommendation.

At last, she was finished packing.

Slowly, she eased the door open, listened for sounds and heard only the faint clatter of pots and pans rising from the kitchen.

Ridiculous, to steal out of the *castello* like a teenager breaking curfew, but she didn't want to answer questions. Not now. Once she was out of here, she'd phone Stefano, thank him for everything, explain that she'd had to get away, that she couldn't impose on him another minute.

Getting her suitcase down the stairs was hard work. She was weaker than she'd thought and by the time she got to the door that led out to the garden, she was light-headed and shaking. Still, she noticed how handsome the *castello* was. The huge expanses of glass were warm and inviting, and heightened the drama of ancient stone walls that spoke of power and isolation.

When the door swung shut behind her, Fallon dropped the suitcase, sank down on it and took half a dozen deep breaths. She felt woozy but there was no time to waste.

Stefano could come back any minute.

She waited until her heart stopped pounding, then rose to her feet. She'd arranged for the taxi to meet her near the gatehouse in an hour. There were still more than thirty minutes to spare.

Far above, a seabird cried out as it flew across the bright blue sky. Fallon looked up, shaded her eyes with her hand, followed the bird until it was barely visible over the water.

That was what she wanted to do. Go down to the sea, feel the warm Mediterranean sun on her skin, let the silken water lap over her toes.

If she moved quickly, she'd have just enough time.

Fallon slipped off her sandals and ran to the path that led down to the rocky beach. The sun was at its zenith; it beat down on her with an almost brutal force as she made her way down the cliff. She still felt light-headed, even a little dizzy, but the sense of freedom was intoxicating and when she reached the beach, she walked into the water, threw back her head, held open her arms and drew the warm, sweet air deep into her lungs as if it were a life force that could heal her, not her face but her heart, her soul...

"*Ma e pazzo!* Are you crazy?"

The familiar male voice was sharp with rage and accompanied by the sound of falling stone.

Fallon swung around and saw Stefano running down the last few feet of the steep path, his face distorted with anger. She took a quick step back, cried out as she stepped on something sharp, and fell just as he reached her.

"What the hell do you think you're doing?" he roared, and lifted her into his arms.

"Put me down!"

"Put you down? Put you down?" He strode onto the beach holding her, his breathing rapid, his eyes hot and dark. "The place I should put you is over my knee! *Il sole siciliano ha cucinato la tua cervella!*"

"I don't know what you're saying!"

"The Sicilian sun has cooked your brain."

"I'm so glad I asked. How could I have lived without hearing that charming sentiment?" Fallon punched his shoulder. "Now put me down!"

"Where? In the water, so you can drown your troubles?"

"Is that what you think—for God's sake, I wasn't—"

"Or maybe you'd like me to put you down here on the

path so that you can lose your footing and make a long, graceful swoon onto the rocks.''

''That's ridiculous! Do I strike you as the swooning type?''

''You didn't, until a couple of days ago.''

''Owning a castle has gone to your head. Do you think you're some—some feudal lord who can intimidate the serfs?'' He didn't answer, and that enraged her even more. ''Damn it,'' she said, punching him again, ''I told you, put—me—''

''Stop hitting me. One misstep and we'll both end up on those rocks.''

''Let go of me and I'll stop hitting… Hey! Hey, what are you doing?''

''Protecting myself,'' he said grimly, and dumped her over his shoulder.

''You jerk! You goon! You—you medieval son of a—''

Fallon gasped as they reached the top of the cliff and Stefano upended her again, this time dumping her on her feet.

''Just what were you thinking?'' he demanded, holding her by the shoulders, shaking her until her teeth rattled. ''Huh? Answer me, damn it! What's going on in that beautiful but empty head of yours?''

''My head is not empty!''

''No. I didn't think so until now.''

''And it's definitely not beautiful.'' She twisted out of his hands and glared at him. ''Only a blind man would say it was.''

''Is that what this is all about? Do you really think your life is over because you're going to have a couple of scars on your face?''

''A couple of…'' Fallon narrowed her eyes. ''You know what, Stefano? You're a fool!''

She turned and started for the *castello* and for the place where she'd left her suitcase but she'd only taken a few steps before he caught up to her, clasped her arm and spun her toward him.

"You could have been killed. Did you ever think of that?"

"For your information, I went up and down that cliff at least two dozen times the week I worked here. Or have you forgotten that I defiled your precious *castello* while you were—while you were wherever you were that week?"

"I was here, right in my own home, and I don't care how many times you climbed that path, you didn't do it when you'd just come out of a hospital."

"I'm fully recovered from the accident. And what do you mean, you were here? I saw you leaving at the airport the day I arrived."

A muscle knotted in Stefano's jaw. He let go of Fallon and folded his arms over his chest.

"There was a change of plans."

"What? You mean, all the time we were baking in the sun, sweltering under that tent, you were watching the peasants from your castle?"

"Letting you people wander through my home was not part of the arrangement."

"*You* people." Fallon folded her arms, too, and cocked her head. "Yes. I'd almost forgotten what you think of people like me."

"Damn it, how did we get off the subject? I leave you for an hour—sixty miserable minutes—and what do I find when I return? A crazy woman, only a couple of days out of a sick bed, wandering the cliffs."

"I was not in a sick bed. And I wasn't wandering. I was standing on the beach."

"You were knee-deep in the sea."

"I was in water barely over my ankles." Fallon lifted her chin. "And why am I explaining myself to you?"

"What if you'd fallen on the path? If a wave had knocked you down?"

"Oh, for heaven's sake, stop being so dramatic! I'm fine. See?" Fallon held out her arms and turned in a swift circle. "I didn't fall, didn't drown, didn't so much as stub my toe."

"Only because you're lucky. You lie around for two days and then, wham, you set off on a hike!"

"I have not been lying around for two days. If I wandered anywhere, it was around and around your guest suite like a lost soul."

"And whose fault is that?" Stefano's mouth thinned. "Staying locked in your rooms was your choice, not mine."

"*Signore* Lucchesi—"

"Don't call me that. I'm as American as you are."

"Are you? The American men I know wouldn't try to tell me what to do and when to do it."

The muscle in his jaw took another quick jump.

"In that case," he said silkily, "you've been dealing with the wrong ones."

"Oh, give me a break! Just because you have this— this lord of the manor complex—"

"You're pushing your luck," he said softly.

"Not half as far as you've pushed yours. What makes you think you have the right to tell me what to do?"

His eyes narrowed. "Shall I show you?"

His voice was soft as silk, yet she could sense the steel beneath it. Stefano had shown her such tenderness since she'd awakened in the hospital that she'd almost forgotten the man he really was, the man who'd insulted her that first day at the airport and denied Carla and the rest of them access to his castle.

"Fallon?"

She blinked. He'd closed the slight distance between them and now he stood only inches from her, so close that she could see that his eyes were a brown so dark they were almost black.

A curl of heat licked through her blood.

How would he prove his right to show a woman who held the power in a relationship with him? By taking her in his arms and proving his strength with his kisses, his caresses, his body?

The thought, so unexpected, so primitive, so unlike her, sent color shooting to her face. She stepped back, raised her chin and looked straight into his chocolate-colored eyes.

"You've been kind," she said calmly, though her heart was racing. "And generous. But if you think that gives you the right to make decisions for me, you're wrong."

"My apologies," he said stiffly. "Of course, you're free to do as you like."

"It's not that I'm ungrateful—"

"I don't want your gratitude."

"Well, you have it anyway." Fallon cleared her throat. "Actually—actually, I've been thinking…"

"And?"

"And, I've decided it's time I left."

His mouth twisted. "Ah. I suppose that explains the suitcase artfully hidden behind the flower bushes."

She felt color rush into her face. "I thought—I figured it was best to leave while you were gone."

"Because?" Stefano tucked his hands into the pockets of his jeans. "Did you think I'd bolt the doors and raise the drawbridge if you told me you wanted to leave?"

"Of course not. It just seemed—um, it seemed simpler that way." She looked at his face, the cool amusement etched across his mouth and in his eyes, and felt a rush of anger. "Damn it, don't laugh at me! All right. I thought you might try to convince me to stay."

"With what? A trip to the dungeon? Whips and chains?"

"I just wanted to avoid a scene, okay? I could imagine you trying to make me believe I was better off here, at *Castello Lucchesi*, than anywhere else."

He nodded, rocked back on his heels and gave her a look that said he found all this vaguely interesting.

"And how would I try to do that?"

"Well…well, you'd say—you'd say this was a perfect place to recuperate."

"Because it's peaceful? Because it's away from those who might stare at you?"

Her face grew hot. "You're blunt."

"I'm honest, and please don't tell me that's not a concern of yours."

"Why would I do that?" she snapped. The freshening wind snatched at her hair and blew it across her face. She scooped it back and tucked it behind her ear. "I mean, you seem to know everything about me."

"I thought I did."

"Which only goes to prove the size of your ego! You've only known me for a little more than a week—"

"I watched you."

She stared at him. "Excuse me?"

"I watched you." This time, it was his face that was suddenly striped with color. "When you were here with the others."

"You? You were the man who…? But why?"

"I'd never seen a shoot before. It was—interesting."

Fallon laughed. She could imagine him finding a photographic safari in Kenya interesting, but a fashion shoot?

"Try again," she said, and the color on his cheeks deepened.

"All right." His voice roughened. "The truth is, I didn't give a damn about the others, or what they were doing. I only saw you."

A little tremor danced up her spine.

"I knew someone was watching," she said softly. "I felt eyes on me. I saw someone… I thought it was one of the castle's security guards."

"Well, it wasn't. It was me."

"And—and why did you watch me?"

"Because you were beautiful," he said bluntly. "And serene, and filled with life…and yet, all the time, I felt you were searching for something."

His words, spoken so quietly, stunned her. How could he have made judgments about her without even speaking to her? And yet, he was right. Those qualities—her serenity, her vitality—were the very ones her agency often used to describe her.

As for the rest…he was right about that, too. She *was* searching for something. For someone. But none of those things applied to her anymore. They described the woman she'd been, not the one she'd be from now on.

Suddenly this talk, this argument, seemed pointless.

"You have a vivid imagination," she said carelessly. "Anyway, I might have been those things before but everything's different now." She turned away. "Thank you for all you've done, but it's time I left."

"It would be foolish to pretend some things about you aren't different," he said, clasping her wrist and trying to make her look at him. When she stood her ground, he stepped in front of her. "Fallon," he said softly, "look at me." Gently, he lifted her face to his. Tears glittered in her eyes and he fought back the desire to kiss them away.

"What's inside you, those qualities in your heart and soul, all the things that make you you, haven't changed." His gaze moved slowly over her face, lingering on her slightly parted lips before meeting her eyes again. "And you're still beautiful."

"No! I've seen myself in the mirror. You can't lie to me, Stefano. I know what I look like."

"You need time to heal. You know what the doctor said. It's impossible to judge what your cuts will be like until the swelling goes down and the stitches come out."

"Look at me," she said fiercely. "Go on, damn it! Take a long, hard look. Do you think what you see is going to vanish just because the stitches come out?"

"Do you really think scars can change the sweetness of your smile, the wisdom I see in your eyes? All you need is time to accept yourself."

"How can I accept someone I don't know?" The tremulous admission freed the tears she'd managed to choke back. They ran down her cheeks as she wound her fingers tightly through his. "Don't you understand? I'm not me anymore!"

"What's inside you is the same," Stefano insisted. "You're too bright to believe that the faces we show the world are our real selves."

"Two weeks ago, I'd have agreed with you. Something like that is easy to say when you look in the mirror and see someone you've always known but now I see—I see—"

Her voice broke. He mouthed an oath in Sicilian and drew her into his arms, held her tight against him until she sobbed and leaned into his body.

"I look at myself," she whispered, "and I see a stranger."

Stefano tucked her head under his chin. Her hair smelled of the salty sea and of the flowers that grew in the castle garden. He wanted to kiss her; he wanted to shake her. Instead, he held her close and rocked her in his arms.

"I know it can be difficult to see beyond what once was," he murmured. "When I first came here, to *Castello Lucchesi,* I saw only ruins. Lost dreams. Hopeless illusions. I couldn't understand why my grandfather had always talked of the *castello* as if the centuries hadn't changed it." He pulled back just enough so he could frame her face with his hands and look down into her eyes. "I decided he'd been filled with an old man's foolishness." He smiled, gently ran his thumb over her soft underlip. "Then I walked the cliffs. I listened to the wind whispering through the fallen stones. And I understood that what had made the castle great was still here, would always be here. I had only to look deep enough to see it.''

Fallon drew a shuddering breath.

"What if you'd walked the cliffs, searched deep within yourself and—and found nothing?'' The wind was as soft as her voice. ''What if you'd discovered that what everyone thought was here had been just an illusion?''

Stefano's eyes dropped to her mouth again. One taste, that was all. One delicate savoring, and he gave in to need, bent his head and kissed her with such tenderness that she felt her heart stand still.

"I've seen a lot of things in my life. I know what is truth and what is illusion. The house I built here is an illusion. Its true beauty comes from the power of the stones that were once part of a real *castello*.'' A muscle knotted in his jaw. ''Your true beauty comes from deep inside you. Nothing can change it.''

Fallon swallowed past the lump in her throat. Oh, she wanted to believe him! Wanted to think that her face had never been anything but a mask...

"Stay here,'' Stefano said quietly. ''Let me help you.''

"You have a life to go back to. People who need you.''

"I have a life I created and people who jump when I speak.'' He smiled, stroked dark strands of silky hair away from her cheeks. ''They can jump just as well from four thousand miles away.''

She laughed, really laughed, for the first time since the accident had stolen her from herself.

"Spoken like a true feudal lord.''

"Is there anything you have to go back to that can't wait a few weeks? People who will worry about you?''

Fallon shook her head. She'd deliberately not contacted her family. Her mother had a weakened heart; her brothers and sisters had their own lives to deal with and besides, she didn't want the entire O'Connell clan rushing to her side, smothering her with well-meant love and sympathy. Not yet.

"A man?"

She looked up. Stefano's eyes were dark.

"No," she said. "There's no one."

"There is now," he said huskily and this time, when his gaze fell like a caress on her mouth, she cupped his jaw and drew his lips down to hers.

CHAPTER SIX

COULD a woman sink into a man's kiss?

Yes, Fallon thought, oh yes, she could.

She wanted to drown in the heat of Stefano's mouth, let her body melt into his. She wanted his hands on her breasts, his teeth on her skin, his mouth between her thighs.

She wanted all of that, now. Here, on the cliff overlooking the sea, with the scent of flowers mingling with the scent of saltwater. This man, this stranger, had become her friend. Her protector.

Now, he would be her lover. And she—she would become flame in his arms.

He groaned against her mouth, a sound of hot, unbridled passion. His body was hard against hers, his kisses soft and sweet even as he nipped her bottom lip between his teeth.

He wanted her as she wanted him; they'd been building to this from the moment they met and now—now it was time.

His hands lifted, cupped her breasts. His fingers skimmed over the light cotton that covered her yearning flesh and she hissed at the exquisite ache of desire that flashed from her nipples to her loins.

"Stefano," she whispered, and he said her name, took the kiss deeper until she was filled with him, with his taste. He trailed his hands down her body, bunched her skirt in one fist, slid his fingers under her fragile summer skirt, up and up her thighs, setting flashfires where he touched her.

Fallon moaned. She raised her leg and wound it high around his.

He was burning her. Melting her. Killing her with his touch, his kisses, his hands.

"Stefano," she said again, "please. Oh please…"

"Yes," he said, his mouth against her throat as her head fell back. "Yes," he said again and he cupped her between her thighs and she cried out, knowing he could feel exactly what he was doing to her, that her heat and wetness were kissing his palm.

This was what she'd longed for. Always, not just the past days or weeks but forever, from the start of time, from the first heartbeat of the universe…

And then, without warning, his arms dropped away from her. She was standing alone, shivering with the sudden chill of his rejection, and when she blinked her eyes open, she saw him looking at her as if he'd never seen her before.

"God," he said roughly, "what are we doing?"

Fallon's throat tightened with pain.

Stefano was staring at her through eyes that were dark, but not with passion. They were dark with shock. With pity. With distaste, and she knew, God, she knew that he'd suddenly realized what he was doing…and who he was doing it with.

How else would a man look at her now? Even this man, who had been so kind.

She wanted to weep. To curse. To slam her fists against his chest and hate him—but how could she, when she understood?

She was grotesque.

And now that she'd flung herself into Stefano's arms, she was something even worse.

She was pathetic.

"Forgive me," he said roughly. "I didn't mean…"

"No." Fallon could feel herself shaking. She wrapped her arms around herself and drew a deep, deep breath. "No," she repeated, "of course you didn't."

"Fallon." He held out his hand. She glanced at it, shook her head and took a quick step back.

"It's all right, Stefano. I understand."

"I'm sorry."

"Yes. So am I." She forced herself to look up, to meet his eyes as she searched for something to say before she fled. "It was—it was just something that happened. I mean, I didn't… I had no intention of…" God, oh God, she wanted to die! "It's been such a strange couple of weeks…"

"For me, too," he said quickly, grabbing the lifeline she'd tossed. "Otherwise, I'd never—"

"I know. Neither would I."

"I wouldn't have—have taken advantage of you that way."

She nodded. He was being a gentleman, taking the blame for her humiliating loss of control when they both knew that his kiss had been affectionate, that she was the one who'd dragged his head down to hers and turned the kiss into something hot and dangerous.

"We'll just—we'll forget this happened," she said, forcing a smile to her lips. "All right?"

He nodded, his eyes still locked to hers, the look of pity so obvious that she wanted to weep.

How would she ever be able to face him again?

"Well." She cleared her throat. "I, uh, I appreciate our talk."

"Our…? Oh. That."

"That. Yes. And—and you're right. I have to start facing the world again."

Stefano nodded. He didn't seem capable of saying anything sensible, and that made nodding his head like one of those damned plastic toys the safest bet.

How in hell could he have done this? Lost control, pawed a woman still weak from an accident that had changed her life? He'd meant only to reassure her, let her know that he cared for her, that he'd take care of her. Instead, he'd come on to her with all the subtlety of a bull moose in rut.

What kind of man made a move on a woman who kept telling him how grateful she was for all his kindness and understanding? Damn it, he didn't want her returning his kisses out of gratitude, he wanted her to respond to him because she wanted him, but how could she know what she wanted when the wounds to her soul were so new?

She'd come a long way but she was still fragile, still vulnerable. What son of a bitch would take advantage of her in that condition?

When she was healed, both outside and in, he'd take her in his arms again, tell her that he wanted to make love to her, to change that look of thankfulness in her eyes to a look of deepest passion…

"…not tonight."

He blinked, focused his eyes on Fallon and realized she was slowly backing toward the house.

"Sorry?"

"I said, I'll think about everything we discussed. You know. Your advice. And—and we'll talk again, but not—"

"Fine. We can talk in the morning." He smiled. Not an easy thing to do, when you'd made such an ass of yourself moments before. What in *hell* had he been thinking? "Join me for breakfast."

"Oh, no. I mean, Anna will bring my breakfast to my room, the way she always—"

"She won't."

Fallon lifted her eyebrows. "Excuse me?"

He'd spoken without thinking but now that he had, he knew it was the right thing to say.

"I'm going to tell her that you'll be taking your meals downstairs from now on. With me."

The look of horror on her face almost made him laugh. His elegant PA had once come to work wearing one brown shoe and one black one. When she'd realized it, Paula had looked the same way Fallon did now.

"That's not possible," she said quickly. "I mean—I mean, I'm not quite up to—"

"Is eight too early for breakfast?"

"If I were going to eat breakfast, eight would be fine, but I never—"

"Anna told me. Black coffee, right?"

Fallon cocked her head. "*Anna* told you?"

"Yes. Coffee for breakfast, a lettuce leaf for lunch—"

"She told you," she repeated, her tone gone icy, "as in, your housekeeper's been reporting my habits to you?"

Stefano shrugged his shoulders. "I wouldn't put it that way."

"No?" She folded her arms. Being angry at him for his smug arrogance was safer than standing here and wishing the ground would open up and swallow her. "Well, I would. And I repeat, I'd rather eat upstairs."

"And *I* repeat, you'll be taking your meals with me."

Fallon narrowed her eyes. What was that old saying about leopards not changing their spots? She'd pegged Stefano Lucchesi right on Day One. Too bad his angel of mercy disguise hadn't lasted.

"I don't take orders very well, *signore*. Perhaps we'd both be better off if I kept that appointment I made with a taxi."

His smile was slow and taunting. "Did you have an appointment, *signorina?* Strange, considering that I haven't seen or heard a car since we've been out here."

Now that she thought about it, neither had she. Fallon

frowned and looked at her watch. More than an hour had gone by since the cab was supposed to meet her at the gate…

Slowly, she lifted her head.

"Your guards turned my cab away," she said flatly.

"They have their orders. Nobody comes in, without my permission…"

"And nobody goes out. Is that the message?"

Stefano shrugged again, a casual lift of the shoulders that made her want to slap him.

"It's the only way I can ensure my privacy." He paused. "And yours…or do you really think no one's likely to discover that the woman who ran off the road on a rainy night and the woman who's a world-famous model are one and the same?"

She felt the color drain from her face. *"Paparazzi?"*

"Sicily is a hotbed of gossip and there've been some rumors. I assumed you wouldn't want to deal with them yet."

"No. No, I wouldn't. I haven't even notified my family."

"Do you want me to do it for you?"

"I'll do it when—when I'm ready."

"In that case," he said gently, "my orders to the guards will stand. Yes?"

"Yes," Fallon said, and it wasn't until hours later, after she was tossing and turning and trying, without success, to fall asleep, that she wondered if she hadn't been manipulated yet one more time by a man who was an expert at the game.

It seemed to come down to a choice between having Anna file reports with Stefano and letting the lord of the manor take mealtime notes himself.

Fallon opted for the latter. Besides, there was always the possibility he'd storm the guest suite and carry her downstairs if she didn't go willingly, and she wasn't about to end up in his arms again.

They had breakfast at eight, lunch at one, dinner at eight and stilted conversation accompanied each meal. During the day, Stefano went into his study; she walked along the cliffs, along the beach—*Let him just try and stop me,* she thought the first time she made the climb down— and in the evenings, she retreated to her sitting room and he...

She had no idea what he did in the evenings.

Most nights, she'd hear the roar of his Harley leaving at nine, then hear it again as he returned long hours later. He probably had a woman in some little hill town; a man like him wouldn't be without a woman for very long. She knew a lot about him now, thanks to a surreptitious trip to his study one evening after he'd gone out.

She knew she didn't belong there. Stefano never invited her inside, not that she expected him to. Not even Anna went past the heavy mahogany doors, but she was going crazy with boredom. There was only so much satellite TV you could watch before your brain turned to mush, she'd told herself as she stepped across the threshold.

Knowing she was in his *sanctum sanctorum* made her heart pound just a little, but the room wasn't what she'd expected. It wasn't Bluebeard's lair; it wasn't an opulent Playboy knockoff. It was just a room, handsomely paneled and carpeted, and furnished with leather chairs, a desk and an assortment of office equipment—a computer, a fax machine, a couple of printers—that explained how Stefano could stay away from New York and his office for weeks at a time.

And there were pictures on the walls.

Stefano, looking very young, grinning broadly as he stood beside a white-haired man with his same handsome features. The grandfather he'd talked about, she assumed.

Stefano, wearing a hard hat, smiling into the camera as

part of a group of half a dozen other hard-hatted men, all of them looking pleased with themselves against a familiar backdrop of sea and sky she recognized as the view right outside the castle.

There were magazines, too, and newspapers, and a quick flip through the stack verified what she'd already dredged out of her knowledge of New York's movers and shakers: Stefano Lucchesi was *the* Stefano Lucchesi, the one who'd created a corporation from the ground up and built a personal fortune that made the most jaded bankers drool.

Fallon took a last look around. Then she switched off the light and left the room. Everything she'd seen confirmed that Stefano was exactly as she'd pegged him. He had a decent streak—the way he'd treated her was proof of that—but, at heart, he was gorgeous, rich as Midas, and, she was certain, hell on women.

Not her, Fallon reminded herself as she went up the stairs. She was immune to that kind of man. She'd lost interest in them after she'd realized some men collected beautiful women the way others collected stamps…

And then she remembered that she didn't need immunity anymore, that she was no longer a woman a man like Stefano would look at more than once, and she went into her room, closed the door after her, went out on the balcony and stared out over the dark, dark sea.

On the fourth morning of their new arrangement, Stefano looked at her over the rim of his coffee cup.

"Are you ready?" he said.

"Ready for what?" Fallon said, startled.

"You have an appointment with the doctor."

Her heart fluttered. Did she? She'd pretty much managed to force all that out of her head. She wore dark glasses, even in the house; she let her hair fall over her face.

She caught Stefano frowning sometimes when he looked at her and she was never sure if it was because he thought she was trying too hard to hide herself or because he wished she'd do a better job of it.

In either case, she wasn't prepared for the bright lights of a hospital or even a trip out the gates of *Castello Lucchesi*.

"Did you forget?"

"Yes," she said politely, "I did. Do you have his number? I'll call and cancel."

Stefano pushed his plate away. "Why?"

"Why what?"

He looked up, his eyes narrowed. "Why would you cancel your appointment?"

"Well—well, I'm feeling fine. There's no need to—"

"Today's the day the stitches come out."

Her belly knotted. "The stitches…"

"Yes." His voice gentled. "It's a big day for you."

Fallon dropped her hands in her lap and curled them into fists.

"I'll go some other time."

"Nonsense," he said briskly, and shoved back his chair. "Tell you what. After you've seen the doctor, we'll celebrate by having lunch at a little restaurant I know. They do a cold seafood salad that's—"

"I'm not ready," she said in a small voice.

Stefano wanted to pull her from her chair, gather her into his arms, hold her and kiss her and tell her that he wasn't ready, either, not for the damned stitches to come out but for her to leave him once they were and she looked at herself and realized that she was scarred, yes, but that in some crazy way, she was more beautiful than ever…

"I'll be with you," he said softly, and she looked up and smiled at him in a way she hadn't done in days, not since he'd come close to ruining things by coming on to her too hard, too fast, too soon. "I'll be with you every

step of the way,'' he said, and he rose to his feet, held
out his hand, and felt his heart lift with joy when she
hesitated and then put her hand in his.

Unfortunately, the doctor had other plans.

"No," he said firmly, when Stefano said he would stay
in the examining room while the doctor took out the
stitches. "Take a walk, *signore*. Get a cup of *espresso*.
The *signorina* and I want to talk."

Whatever they'd talked about hadn't done much good.
Stefano knew that the second the nurse said he could go
back into the examining room. Fallon sat on a high stool,
her body rigid, her face turned away from him.

The doctor took him by the arm and walked him into
the hall.

"We were very lucky," the doctor told him. "There
was no infection, no distortion, no raised ridges of angry
flesh."

"But?"

The doctor sighed, took off his glasses and polished
them on the hem of his white jacket.

"But, she refuses to deal with reality."

"You can hardly blame her for that, Doctor. Did you
know she was a model? That her face was her career?"

"Do you want to see her make a complete recovery,
Signore Lucchesi? Or do you want to keep her dependent
on you?"

"Be careful what you say to me, *Signore* Dottore,"
Stefano growled, but the doctor was unmoved by his
warning.

"It's inadvertent, of course, but you're doing it all the
same. The *signorina* is made of strong stuff but it would
be simple for her to hide in a cocoon if you are too generous with your compassion."

"I haven't done that! Did she tell you that she locked

herself away in her room? That I all but forced her to come downstairs and sit at my table for meals?''

"Has she gone anywhere else? To the store, to a café, even out for a drive?''

Stefano sagged back against the wall. "What are you suggesting? That I shove her into public, demand she show her face to the world when I see how it hurts her even to look at herself?''

"What I suggest," the doctor said gently, "is that you help her move forward." He put his hand lightly on Stefano's arm. "The lady is healed on the outside—now, she must heal in a far more difficult place. Inside her heart, where the pain hurts the most.''

Going home, Fallon sat silently in the car, hidden behind dark glasses and a floppy-brimmed straw hat.

"Everything went very well," Stefano finally said.

She didn't answer.

"The doctor says—''

"I don't want to talk about it." She fell silent. Then she gave a bitter little laugh. "The irony of it is that I'd been thinking and thinking, the last few months, about what else I'd like to do with my life.''

"And?''

"What do you mean, and? I didn't think I'd have to make the decision in an instant.''

"But you've given it some thought...?''

"How could I?" she said sharply. "Don't you get it? Everything's changed.''

The car pulled through the gates of the *castello* and glided to a stop at the front door. Stefano said something to his driver, got out and opened Fallon's door himself. She moved quickly past him and he went after her, put his hands on her shoulders and skimmed them down her arms, to her wrists.

More than anything he'd ever done, he wanted to help her. Part of it was for her but he knew that if he were honest, part of it, maybe the biggest part, was purely, self-ishly, for himself.

He felt something he couldn't name for this woman. Hell, he wasn't ready to give it a name, or even look at it too closely, but it was there and he knew he didn't have a chance in hell of figuring out what it was until she was whole again.

"I understand," he said carefully, "that you won't get better until you accept what's happened to you."

She gave him a look that said he was crazy. "Do I have a choice?"

"*Cara*. There's a difference between acceptance and sufferance."

Her eyes narrowed on his. "Here we go. Philosophy 101, Sicilian style."

"I've told you repeatedly, I am not—"

"You are. I can hear what happens, that—that change in the cadence of your words, the way you suddenly have of sounding as if you're a font of old-world wisdom."

It wasn't true. He was trying to help her, she knew, but the only way he could do that would be to say, *You don't need those glasses or that hat. Yes, your face is scarred but I can see past those scars. I want you, anyway. I've always wanted you, even before I met you...*

She took a gulp of air.

Hadn't they said she'd suffered a mild concussion? Maybe that was why she was thinking such irrational thoughts. She didn't want Stefano, didn't need him, didn't need anyone to lean on. She never had and never would. Her mother had leaned all over her father and where had it gotten her? Dragged all around the country, that was where, while his wife and kids made the best of a bad situation.

Besides, she'd already embarrassed herself with this man.

No way in the world was it going to happen again.

"Never mind," she said. "It doesn't matter."

"Fallon. Look, I don't want to quarrel with you—"

"Then keep quiet."

"Can't we have a civil conversation?"

"No."

She was impossible! Fire and steel and silk, all in one package.

He didn't want to quarrel, he wanted to talk. No, he didn't want that, either. What he really wanted was to haul her into his arms, kiss her senseless, tell her that he'd already figured out what she would do with her life. She would spend it with him.

He swallowed hard.

What he had to do was be calm. Rational. Convince her to be the same way. They *would* talk, the way they'd managed to do for a little while the day he'd found her on the beach.

It was just that he wasn't good at reading women unless it involved simple things, like when they asked you if a dress made them look heavy. *No.* Or if this hairstyle was attractive. *Yes.* Or if he'd like to leave a change of clothes in the closet or a razor in the medicine cabinet, in which case he always knew what to say and how to say it so that his answer was as polite and painless as possible.

This situation was new to him. He needed to tell a woman the truth in a way that would help her, and how did a man do that?

"I'm just trying to point something out to you, Fallon."

She lifted her chin. He could see the warning in the gesture. *You're on thin ice,* she was saying.

"And that would be…?"

"Feeling sorry for yourself won't help."

Damn it! Of all the stupid things to say! He could see her turn rigid with anger.

"I didn't mean—"

"The hell you didn't!" Face white, she tore her hands free of his.

"So, you think I'm wallowing in self-pity."

"I didn't say that."

"You didn't have to. It's what you think."

"I don't." He hesitated. "But even if you were," he said, choosing his words with extravagant care, "feeling sorry for oneself would be natural, given the circumstances."

"This has nothing to do with *one*self," Fallon said, jabbing her thumb against her chest, "it is to do with *my*self! With me, not you and not some—some saint who'd probably look in the mirror and say oh, how wonderful, look what's happened to me!"

"Fallon. *Cara…*"

"Do not *'cara'* me!" She swung away from him, strode toward the house, then turned back. "Do you want to hear a funny story, Stefano? I've got a great one. The doctor was called away for a couple of minutes right before he took out my stitches. His nurse brought me a couple of magazines to leaf through, while I waited for him to come back. And I opened one of them and turned a few pages and you know what I saw?" Her mouth twisted. "Me. Me, looking like a human being instead of a freak."

Stefano fought the desire to drive back to the hospital, find the nurse and pry open her skull to see if she really had a brain inside it.

"I'm sorry that happened to you, but—"

"And then Dr. Frankenstein comes in and expects me to ooh and ahh over his wonderful job of cut and paste!"

"Fallon. Please—"

"I'm going home tomorrow."

"And do what? Lock yourself in your apartment?"

"What I do is my business!"

Fallon turned her back. Stefano grabbed her arm and spun her toward him.

"That's it," Stefano said grimly. *"Basta!"*

"At least we agree on something. *Basta,* indeed. Enough is exactly right. You are not my keeper, and don't bother giving me that speech about the Chinese and their inane proverbs."

"Have you looked in the mirror?" He caught her by the elbows and shook her. "Answer me! Have you looked?"

"I don't have to look. I see everything I need to in your face."

"What?"

She twisted out of his grasp, flew into the house and up the stairs, and all he could do was stand there and try to figure out what in hell had just happened.

CHAPTER SEVEN

FALLON dumped her suitcase on the bed, opened the closet and tore her clothes from the shelves and racks.

She should have left here that first time instead of letting Stefano talk her into staying on. She didn't belong here and he certainly didn't belong in her life.

The gall of the man! Who in hell did he think he was, telling her how she should feel and act?

Stefano Lucchesi lived by his own rules in his own private universe. People jumped when he spoke; wasn't that pretty much what he'd said? What he'd boasted, for heaven's sake? He'd probably never had to sweat for an honest day's pay in his pampered, self-centered life.

How could he possibly understand what it was like to have one of the most sought-after faces in the world one minute and the next—the next—

Fallon dumped an armful of shoes into the suitcase.

His world was secure. Hers was a blur, it had been turned upside down by a bored god with an eye for black comedy. She'd lost her career.

Far worse, she'd lost her sense of self.

All those articles in women's magazines about finding yourself... She'd always thought it the height of self-indulgence to waste energy gazing at your own navel, but now—but now—

Her mouth trembled.

Better to think about Stefano and how mistaken she'd been thinking he had a single bone of compassion in his body.

Did he see her as a charity case? What a fool she'd been to stay here.

Fallon stormed into the bathroom, grabbed the wicker trash basket from the corner and swept the vanity clean of all her makeup and creams and lotions. Half the stuff landed in the basket, the rest on the floor. Tins opened, shadows spilled.

Jasper Johns would have called the resultant mess a work of art.

She thought it fitting.

She didn't need all those stupid tools of her trade—her former trade—anymore. Who would care if she wore the right color lip gloss? Who'd give a damn what kind of mascara she used to darken her lashes?

A woman with a face that could scare little children didn't need makeup, she needed a paper bag.

What she definitely did *not* need were Readings from Oprah as served up by the Lord of the Manor.

Fallon slammed a fist against the marble vanity.

"Stefano Lucchesi," she muttered, "you are a smug, sanctimonious, self-serving, holier-than-thou son of a bitch!"

"Alliterative," she heard a deep voice behind her say in a thoughtful tone, "but untrue. My mother was a very nice woman."

Fallon whirled around. Stefano was lounging in the bathroom doorway, hands tucked casually into his pockets.

"What are you doing in my room?"

"As for sanctimonious, self-serving and—what was that other thing you called me?"

"I said, what—are—you—doing—in—my—room?"

"Holier-than-thou. That was it." Stefano sighed, leaned a shoulder against the doorjamb and crossed one moccasin-clad foot over the other. "Sounds good but it's repetitive, don't you think? Considering that someone who's sanctimonious is those other things, too."

Fallon glared at him. "How dare you barge in here?"

"I didn't barge, I knocked."

"With what? A feather?" she said, blowing the hair from her eyes and folding her arms over her chest. "I certainly didn't hear you."

"Well, you couldn't have. You were making too much noise, stamping your feet and breaking the place up."

Color streaked her cheeks. "I have never stamped my feet in my life. You have a vivid imagination."

Stefano raised one eyebrow and looked down at the tile floor. Fallon looked, too, and her color deepened.

"I was in a hurry. I dropped a few things."

"So it seems. I'll bet there's a king's fortune of magic elixirs there."

"What I do with my stuff is my business."

"I thought women loved all those silly little pots of nonsense."

"It's not nonsense."

"Then why throw them away?"

"I have no use for them anymore."

He gave her a long, indecipherable look. *Go on,* she thought grimly, *I dare you.* One more lecture on Facing Reality and she'd smack him... Or fall into his arms and weep.

Oh, God. Was she that close to tears? Was her mask ready to slip? Quickly, she bent down and began scooping up the scattered cosmetics. Stefano squatted beside her and grabbed her hand.

"Let me do that."

"I am perfectly capable of cleaning up after my own messes."

"I'm sure you are," he said calmly, "but there's nothing wrong with accepting a little help."

That wasn't a topic she wanted to pursue. Instead, Fallon gave him a scathing look, reached for the basket and began dumping makeup into it.

Stefano picked up a little container of eye shadow.

"Caramel Crème Sundae?"

"If you think it's your shade," Fallon said sweetly, "be my guest."

"And Wild Honey Mousse," he said, plucking a tube of lip gloss from the floor. He looked up, his eyes meeting hers. "Why is it these things always sound like the menu in a bad French restaurant?"

"Give me that," Fallon demanded, snatching the gloss from him and tossing it into the trash. "And go away. I told you, I don't need your help."

"You need someone's," he said quietly. Before she could respond, he scooped up almost all the remaining containers and tossed them in the basket. "I'm almost done."

Glaring, Fallon sat back on her heels. He was right; he'd finished the job. He could pick up several of the little pots and tubes at one time. The stuff looked like sample sizes in his big hands.

Such capable, comforting hands.

Fallon shot to her feet. "Thank you," she said stiffly.

"You're welcome."

"And I'm sorry if I made so much noise it bothered you."

"I didn't hear a thing until I was right outside the door."

"Then why—"

"I came to apologize."

She blinked. "Apologize?"

"Right."

Stefano brushed off his hands, then wiped them on the seat of his jeans. It was crazy, but the simplicity of the gesture was disarmingly boyish.

"I was an ass," he said.

"I beg your pardon?"

"You heard me. Telling you how I thought you should handle things was wrong."

Fallon stared at him. Did he really think an apology would erase her memories of his arrogance?

"In fact," he said with a little smile, "I was a sanctimonious, self-serving, holier-than-thou ass."

She didn't want to smile, but how could she prevent her lips from curving just a little bit?

"Close, wasn't I?"

Stefano grinned. "Yeah, but close only counts in horseshoes and hand grenades." His smile tilted. "Seriously, I was dead wrong. What happened to you was hell. You're the only one who can possibly know the emotional cost involved."

He really did look sorry for what he'd said. All things considered—he'd stayed with her every moment in the hospital, brought her to his home to recover—she supposed she could bend a little and accept his apology.

Besides, she was leaving the *castello* soon. Surely, under those circumstances, it was simple good manners to forgive a man who was willing to admit he was a jerk.

"I didn't mean to hurt you," he said softly. "You must know that I'd never do that."

Their eyes met and held.

No, Fallon thought, he wouldn't. He'd meant well and if she were to be brutally honest, he'd given her advice she knew, in her heart, she needed to take. Wallowing in self-pity, hiding from the world, wasn't going to change the past any more than it would help move her into the future.

Stefano reached out a hand, as if to touch her. Then he pulled it back and cleared his throat.

"I'll leave you alone now. But if you change your mind, if you want company or someone to talk to…" He smiled. "Or if you'd like a target to throw things at, all you have to do is—"

"You were right."

She knew she'd blurted the words in one quick rush,

but how else could she have gotten them out of her mouth?

"What?"

Fallon swallowed hard. "I said, you were right." She looked at the floor, at her feet, anywhere but at his face. "I've been drowning in self-pity."

"No," he said quickly. "That's not true. I was wrong to imply it. I only meant—"

"Self-pity. And denial." Fallon took a deep breath and looked up. "I keep thinking, if I hadn't been on that road, if it hadn't started to rain…" She caught her bottom lip, worried it between her teeth. "I know that thinking that way is a waste of time."

"It isn't, when it's a part of healing. That's what I overlooked."

She smiled a little. "When I was little, I broke my arm riding my brother's bike. It was a dumb thing to do—the bike was much too big for me and I knew it. Afterward, when I found out I'd have to wear a cast for almost the entire summer, I moaned and groaned and finally my mother said, *Fallon, my girl, if you'd put half the energy into getting on with things as you're putting into regretting them, you'd be a whole lot happier.*"

Stefano grinned. "Are you sure your mother isn't Italian? That's pretty much the same speech my grandmother made when I ran home crying because Mr. Rienzi caught me stealing a water pistol from his store and boxed my ears."

"You? A thief?" She smiled again. "I'd never have believed it!"

"Hey, it was the price of initiation into the Mott Street Mohicans."

"The Mott Street…?"

Fallon laughed. Really laughed, and the sound went straight through him, from the top of his head to the tips of his toes. So far, he could count on one hand the number of times he'd seen her laugh since the accident. What he wanted, more than anything, was to hear that sweet sound, see her eyes light, all the time.

"Uh-huh. What can I tell you? It was summer, we'd been playing cops and robbers and I'd already blown my allowance on candy and comic books. How can a cop catch a robber without a gun?"

"Plus, swiping a toy was a rite of passage?"

"I think getting your ears boxed and your backside warmed was the actual rite of passage."

They both smiled this time, and then Fallon's smile wavered.

"The thing is, my mother would probably have told me exactly what you did this afternoon. I need to look ahead, not back."

"I'm glad to hear you say that," Stefano said softly. He moved closer, reached out and tucked her hair behind her ear.

"I wasn't angry at you, I was angry at myself. You—you've been wonderful. Kind and generous and compassionate." Her lips curved in a smile. "Not alliterative, but true."

He smiled, too, and slipped his arms around her.

"You're a remarkable woman, Fallon O'Connell."

Fallon's eyes blurred with tears. "I'm not," she said, shaking her head as she leaned against him. "I'm a mope."

Stefano chuckled. "If you are, you're a beautiful mope."

"Please don't lie to me, Stefano. I know what I look like."

He bent his head and pressed a kiss into the silkiness of her dark hair.

"Then you know that your eyes are the color of the sea," he said softly, "that your mouth is as pink and soft as the petals of a rose." He framed her face with his hands and raised it to his. "And you know that the woman you really are is as whole as she was before that accident, and that she's more lovely than any man deserves.''

His words swept through her like sweet fire. She met his eyes, and when his gaze dropped to her mouth, she sighed his name and parted her lips as he kissed her.

His arms tightened around her, brought her tightly against his body so that she could feel the hardness of his erection. Desire quickened her heartbeat; she said his name again and wound her arms around his neck.

''Fallon,'' he whispered against her mouth, ''Fallon, *belissima*.''

He kissed her again, and she began to tremble, stunned with the intensity of her need. She'd never felt this way in the arms of a lover, never wanted to give this much, to take this much. The realization terrified her; she stiffened and pulled back.

''I can't. Stefano, I'm sorry. I—I—''

She could almost see him fighting for self-control. At last, he smiled and leaned his forehead against hers.

''Do you know that we've never been out on a date?''

''A date?''

''You know. I bring flowers, we go to a special place for supper, we drink champagne, dance in the moonlight...'' He smiled, reached behind his neck, caught her wrists and brought her hands between them, to his chest. ''A date, Fallon.''

Her heart gave a kick. She wasn't ready to face the world. Not yet. Oh, not yet!

''Bella signorina,'' he said solemnly. ''Would you do me the honor of coming out with me tonight?''

''Stefano.'' Fallon slicked the tip of her tongue across her bottom lip. ''I know it's the right thing to do. Going out in public, I mean, but—''

He brought her hands to his mouth, kissed first one and then the other.

''And I know the perfect place. A terrace in a beautiful garden, and just beyond it, a cliff that overlooks the sea.''

"Do you mean…here? At the *castello?*"

He kissed her, his mouth moving gently over hers. "The volcano has been restless all week. If we're lucky, she might light the darkness for us tonight."

Fallon smiled. "I'd be honored to have supper with you, *signore.*"

"Seven o'clock, then. I'll be waiting."

She lifted her face to his and when he kissed her this time, she thought that surely the earth must have moved under her feet.

At six, Fallon was standing beside her bed, staring unhappily at the clothing tossed across it.

She'd put everything away, hung the dresses and pants neatly on hangers, folded the shirts and shorts and stacked them on the shelves…and then she'd pulled all of it out again, outfit by outfit, held dresses and blouses and pants against herself as she stared into the mirror and said no, no, no.

Fallon sighed and sank down on the edge of the bed. She'd been on a lot of dates. She knew what to wear to a foreign film at a funky little theater in the Village and how to dress for late supper at the newest bistro. And this was only a dinner at home.

No, it wasn't. This was dinner at a castle, with a man who made her feel things she'd never felt before.

What was the dress code for that?

A summer dress and high heels? A long skirt with a halter top? Sweats and sneakers? She wanted to look right. To make Stefano's eyes light when he saw her. To somehow make him go on thinking she was still beautiful, still desirable…

A light knock sounded at the sitting room door. Fallon rose to her feet, smoothed back her hair and hurried to open it.

"*Signorina? Sono Anna.*"

"Yes, Anna. I didn't ring for any—"

"Scusi," Anna said importantly and pushed a small cart laden with glass vases past Fallon and into the bedroom.

"Scusi," the impassive Luigi mumbled, following on Anna's heels, his arms filled with long, white florists' boxes.

"Excuse *me,"* Fallon said in bewilderment. "What is all this?"

"Fiori," Anna said. *"Fiori, tutti per voi."*

Sicilian or Italian, whichever it was, the meaning was clear. Flowers. Flowers, all for her.

"All of them?" Fallon said, waving her hands.

She watched, stunned, as Luigi opened the boxes and Anna emptied them of their beautiful contents. Yellow roses. Red roses. Black tulips, pale lavender orchids, white hyacinths, purple violets and blue pansies, even an assortment of wildflowers. Anna bustled from sitting room to bathroom to bedroom, filling the vases with water, then with flowers, and arranging them on every available surface.

At last, she smiled at Fallon and handed her a small ivory envelope. She made a shooing motion at Luigi, who dipped his head.

"Signorina," he said politely.

The door swung shut, and Fallon was alone.

She turned in a slow circle, staring at the flowers that filled the sitting room. She went into the bedroom and stared some more.

Then she opened the envelope, took out the note card and read it.

I wanted to send you flowers, but I didn't know which were your favorites.

Scrawled beneath the message was Stefano's signature.

Fallon picked up the yellow roses and buried her face in their soft petals. She'd never had a favorite flower but from now all of these would be.

Smiling even as her eyes filled with tears, she went to the bedroom closet and took out the only garment she'd left hanging in it. Her racing heart told her it was the one thing, the only thing that would complement this night.

CHAPTER EIGHT

By six-forty, Stefano had paced his bedroom and sitting room so many times he was surprised he hadn't worn a hole in the carpet.

At six forty-five, he decided that if he checked his watch again he'd probably rip it off his wrist and hurl it at the wall. Better to check the mirror, run his hands through his hair...

Basta!

He was behaving like a schoolboy.

Briskly, he shut off the light and went down the stairs to the terrace.

Yes. This was better. He could breathe easier out here, where day was already giving way to night. The sky had taken on a delicate translucency; the sea seemed touched with tendrils of gold, and the omnipresent trails of molten lava that flowed down the face of Mount Etna were as bright as ribbons of fire.

Anna had set the terrace table with the *castello's* finest linens, flatware and china. A serving cart stood to the side, laden with covered platters and bowls; a bottle of Cristal champagne stood chilling in a bucket. Everything was ready for the evening.

Everything but him.

He was pacing again, this time back and forth along the terrace. He couldn't recall being so on edge before. He was cool under fire in business; it went without saying he was relaxed in his dealings with women.

People said *il lupo solo* had nerves of steel.

All true…but not tonight.

What if Fallon had changed her mind about accepting his apology?

What if she'd decided against joining him for dinner?

What if she laughed at all those flowers?

He'd never intended to send so many when he phoned the florist.

"I want a dozen yellow roses," he'd said, imagining the color against the ebony of her hair, and then he'd thought, but what if she doesn't like yellow roses?

So he'd ordered red ones, too. And black tulips, to show her that even in somberness there was beauty. And pansies, because Fallon was as down-to-earth as she was elegant, and orchids and hyacinths and now he could only wonder if she was upstairs laughing at him, or staring in the mirror, telling herself she'd made a mistake in agreeing to spend the evening with him at all.

Stefano checked his watch again. It was five after seven. If she didn't show up soon, he was going to take the steps two at a time, push open her door, tell her that he was going crazy and it was all her fault—

"Hello."

He swung toward the terrace doors and felt his heart stand still. Fallon was standing there, a smile trembling on her lips, and she was every dream a man could imagine come to life.

He'd dressed in a tux for the evening. He'd only wanted to create the right setting for her reentry into the world. It hadn't mattered to him what she wore, jeans or a gown.

She'd chosen to wear a gown, a long, slender length of silk that clung to her body, its color a green as deep and pure as her eyes. Her hair was loose, a straight fall of sable into which she'd tucked one delicate yellow rosebud.

"Hello," he said, although he had to clear his throat to get the word out, but maybe it was all right because her smile steadied and she started toward him on impossibly high stiletto heels. He tried not to think about her wearing those heels, that smile, the yellow rose and nothing else.

"I'm sorry I'm late."

Stefano shook his head, moved toward her and reached for her hand.

"*Mia bella*," he said huskily, "how beautiful you are!"

Fallon put her hand in his. "So are you."

He laughed, grateful for the reprieve.

"I've been called many things, but 'beautiful' isn't one of them." He kissed her knuckles, her palm, then tucked her hand into the crook of his arm. "I'm glad you liked the yellow roses."

"All the flowers are wonderful. My rooms look like a garden."

His face felt warm. Was he blushing?

"Well," he said, "I didn't know which ones you'd prefer."

"All of them. It was the loveliest gift anyone's ever given me." She looked up and smiled again. "Thank you."

He looked into her eyes, at her mouth, and wanted to kiss her. Just a light kiss, a way of saying it had been his pleasure to send the flowers, but her scent teased his nostrils, a strand of her hair brushed his cheek, and he felt his body turn hard.

Now he understood why he'd been so edgy all afternoon, why he'd snapped at Anna when she'd asked a simple question about dessert, why he'd snapped at Luigi over an equally simple question about the car, why he'd gone down to the beach and swum far into the sea— farther than he knew was wise—before swimming back to shore.

He wanted Fallon.

That was what this night was all about.

He wanted her in a way he'd never wanted a woman before. He looked into her face, saw both the scars that marked it and the beauty that defined it, and imagined how it would feel to move over her and watch her eyes darken with pleasure as he filled her.

The truth was that this night was less about luring her back into the world than it was about luring her into his bed, and if that didn't qualify him to be the self-serving SOB she'd said he was, it came damned close.

"Stefano?"

He blinked at the soft tone of inquiry, brought his eyes back to focus on her.

"Is something wrong?"

Yes. Something was very wrong. She made him feel things he didn't understand. More than hunger. More than desire.

"No," he said, and cleared his throat, "but there will be, if we let Anna's meal get cold." He slid his arm around her waist, drew her against him and lowered his voice to a stage whisper. "She's thrilled you're dining with me tonight."

A wash of pale pink rose in Fallon's cheeks.

"So am I," she said softly, and the need Stefano felt for her pounded through his blood.

He opened the Cristal and poured it into Baccarat flutes. He served Anna's paper-thin smoked tuna, her *caponata,* the grilled lamb and what she said was a Sicilian specialty, *pasta con le sarde.*

The tuna was like silk, the *caponata* a heavenly mingling of tomato, aubergine and olives. The lamb was delicious and the pasta with fresh sardines dazzled Fallon's taste buds with hints of the sea and of the fennel that grew everywhere on Sicily.

But she managed only a bite of each.

How could she eat when her heart felt lodged in her throat? When Stefano was so gorgeous, so masculine, so funny, so wonderful?

It was a warm night and, after asking her if it was okay

with her, he'd discarded his tie, his jacket, undone the top couple of buttons of his shirt and rolled back his cuffs.

As handsome as he'd been in his tux, he was even more handsome this way. Dark and dangerous and sexy, she thought, and felt her pulse accelerate.

They talked of the New York they both loved, of Sicily, of places they'd seen in their travels. He told her about buying back the land that the *castello* was built on; when he described the elderly Sicilians who'd owned it, he lapsed into a really awful imitation of Marlon Brando doing Vito Corleone, and she burst into giggles.

Stefano's eyes darkened.

"I love the way you laugh," he said, and she thought how long it was since she'd felt so happy. Not just since the accident, she realized, but long before that.

She hadn't felt this filled with life in a very long time.

"Tell me about *Castello Lucchesi*," she said. "About your grandfather."

He shrugged his shoulders, leaned back in his seat and sipped his wine.

"I loved him," he said simply. "He was tough and hard, like this island, and as giving and generous as its people."

"And you built the castle for him."

She said it so simply that he knew she understood.

"Yes. I built it for him. I only wish he'd lived long enough to see it."

Impulsively, she reached for his hand. His fingers closed tightly around hers.

"I'll tell you the story someday. For now, let's just say that revenge can become a way of life for some people." He smiled and squeezed her hand again. "Your turn. Tell me about you."

She said there wasn't much to tell, yet somehow, a quarter of an hour later, she was still talking, telling him about her family, the years spent growing up and moving from place to place while her father searched for ways to make the roll of the dice and the turn of a card pay off.

She told him things she'd never told anyone, how gawky she'd felt in high school when she shot up to five-ten and all the other girls, even her sisters, were inches shorter.

"Height impaired," Stefano said, straight-faced.

He grinned and so did she, and that made her laugh all over again and when she did, he thought how incredible it was to see her laugh so many times in one wonderful evening.

"Meg and Bree caught up, eventually," Fallon said, and suddenly she knew she couldn't manage the pretence much longer. She wanted to be in Stefano's arms, to feel his mouth on hers, and if he didn't touch her soon, she was going to make a fool of herself by throwing herself at a man who was interested in being kind, not in being her lover.

God, what was she thinking?

Fallon sat up straight, put down her fork and touched her mouth with her napkin.

"Well," she said briskly, "it's getting late."

Was it? Yes, Stefano thought in surprise, it must be. A while ago, he'd lit the tall white tapers that stood in the center of the table and the tiny lights strung among the trees in the garden had come on. To the west, the blackness of the night was broken only by the faint lights of scattered houses and by the rivers of fire that streaked the breast of the volcano.

Speakers, hidden in the garden, sent the softest possible music into the flower-scented night.

Beautiful, all of it, but not as beautiful as Fallon.

She was getting to her feet. He didn't want her to go. But she was probably tired. All this—the meal, though neither of them had eaten much; the wine; even the night air must have exhausted her...

Stefano stood up.

"Don't go." She looked at him, her eyes wide and shining, and he felt a fist close around his heart. "You can't leave until we've had our dance. Remember? I asked you to have supper with me and to go dancing."

"I know, but here…?"

"Here. Right here. Right now." His voice had taken on a note of command and then it softened. "Please," he said, and opened his arms.

He saw the little lift of her breasts and knew she'd caught her breath. Would she turn him down? If she did, he'd be a gentleman and let her go.

The hell with that. He hadn't made a fortune by being a gentleman. If she said no, he'd pull her into his arms, bring her soft body against his, stroke his hands over her until she sighed and said yes to dancing with him, yes to making love with him, yes, yes, yes…

"Yes," Fallon whispered, and went into his arms.

He held her close. Put one hand at the base of her spine, curved the other around the nape of her neck, under the lush mantle of her hair. She was tall, taller than ever in those incredible shoes, and that was good because it meant when he brought her head against him, her face tucked just against his shoulder and he felt the warm sigh of her breath against his throat.

Stefano put his lips against her hair. He'd held her before but never like this, with her body pressed against the full length of his, her breasts soft against the hardness of his chest, her long legs molded to his.

He shut his eyes. The music was slow and soft and he began moving to it, holding her close, inhaling her fragrance, feeling himself grow aroused at the sway of her body against his. He wanted her so badly it was agony, feeling her against him, but he didn't want to push her into something she didn't want or wasn't ready for, and he almost laughed as he wondered what the world would think of *il lupo solo* right now, cautious and unsure for the first time in his life.

One kiss, he thought. One taste, and then Fallon whispered his name on a sigh. Stefano looked down into her face, saw eyes that were dark and filled with desire, a mouth that trembled in anticipation of his kiss, and he forgot everything but this woman and this night and what his heart told him they'd both wanted from the first time they'd met.

He bent his head, took her mouth. Her lips parted, opened to his, and he groaned, angled his head, slanted his mouth over hers again and feasted on her taste. She made a little sound, the breathless whisper a woman makes in the moment of her surrender, and he gave up thinking.

His hands skimmed over her, molding her breasts, toying with the tight, erect nipples. Fallon's head fell back and he nipped at her bared throat, kissed the hollow where her pulse raced as rapidly as his.

"Tell me what you want," he whispered, and she cupped his face, brought his mouth to hers.

She didn't answer. For a long, agonizing minute he thought he'd made a mistake, that he wanted her so badly he'd fooled himself into thinking she felt the same way.

Then a tremor went through her and she brought his mouth down to hers.

"You," she said fiercely. "Only you."

He bunched her gown in his hands, pushed it to her hips, thrust one leg between hers and almost lost himself when she cried out and moved against his thigh.

He cupped her bottom, groaned when he felt her warm, naked flesh. She was wearing a thong; the thought of how she must look in the wisp of silk almost drove him to his knees. He slid one hand between her thighs, cupped her mons, felt the heat and wetness of her against his palm and knew he was close to the edge.

Quickly, he scooped her into his arms. She kissed his throat as he carried her up the stairs; when he reached his bedroom, he shouldered the door open, kicked it shut behind him and took her to the bed, setting her down beside it, letting her slide down his body until her feet touched the floor.

"I don't want to hurt you. If it's too much, if you want me to stop—"

She put her hand over his mouth. "I'm not made of glass."

"I know. But—"

She kissed him, her mouth soft and warm. Then she stepped back, her eyes never leaving his, and reached behind her for the zipper that went down the back of her gown.

Stefano caught her shoulders.

"Let me do that," he said in a thick voice.

She lifted her hair and turned her back to him. Slowly, he drew down the zipper, kissing every inch of her spine as he uncovered it. Then he slid down the thin shoulder straps and, in a whisper of silken sibilance, the green silk floated to the floor.

He drew her back against him. She was almost naked now, braless, wearing only the thong and the stiletto heels. He shut his eyes, cupped her breasts, groaned as he felt her nipples thrust against his palms.

"Fallon," he said, and turned her toward him.

God, she was exquisite. High breasts, a slender waist, gently curved hips and legs that went on forever.

And her face, her beautiful, elegant face with its fine bones, chiseled features and on them, the cruel reminders of how close he'd come to losing her before he'd had the chance to know her any place but in his dreams.

"Don't look at me like that," she said, her voice shaking. "My face—"

He caught her wrists as she began lifting her hands, circled them with one hand and clamped them against his chest.

"I want all of you," he said fiercely. "Do you understand? I want everything you were, everything you are, everything you will be." He lowered his head toward her, holding her eyes with his. "I'll give you everything I am, in return. Tell me you agree to that, *bellisima,* because it's the only way it can be for us."

He waited, wondering if he'd pushed too far, demanded too much. Her eyes filled with tears and he thought he had, but before he could gather her close, tell her he would accept whatever she could give, she lifted her mouth to his and kissed him.

Stefano tore off his clothes and dug a small packet from the drawer in the night table. Then he lifted Fallon into his arms and came down with her in the center of the bed.

Slowly, he took off her shoes, pausing to kiss her delicately arched feet, her toes. He kissed her mouth, her breasts, her belly. She moaned and arched toward him and he peeled the thong away so that she lay before him naked, vulnerable, and he knew that he would never want another woman after this night.

He kissed her thighs, her labia, kissed the budding flower hidden there as she sobbed his name. She reached down to stop him but he caught her hands, held them at her sides, kissed and licked until she arched beneath him again and came.

He gathered her to him then, held her, soothed her, kissed her mouth and told her how wonderful she was.

"Stefano," she said, "Stefano, please…"

"Yes, *cara,*" he whispered, and he drew back, parted her thighs and on one long, hard thrust, sheathed himself deep inside her. Fallon cried out his name and he watched with fierce pleasure as another orgasm tore through her. Then she reached up and touched his face, and that gentle caress was his undoing.

Stefano groaned, let go and went with her.

Fallon awoke with a start.

An arm, heavy and possessive, lay curled around her waist; there was a leg draped over hers. Stefano's arm.

Stefano's leg. She was in his room, in his bed. Smiling, she let her head fall back against his shoulder. She must have fallen asleep in his arms.

Something rumbled in the distance. Thunder, she thought, and snuggled closer. Lightning, too; every now and then, it pierced the blackness of the bedroom. Maybe it would rain. She liked rain, and the thought of waking to it in Stefano's arms was...

"Mmm," Stefano said, and wrapped both arms around her.

Fallon touched her hand to his face. His jaw was soft with stubble; she gave a little laugh when he caught the tip of her finger gently between his teeth.

"Hey! That hurts."

"It doesn't."

"It could have."

"Well, it's what you get for waking me. Have you no pity for a man on the brink of collapse?"

She wiggled a little, felt the quick surge of his erection against her belly and reveled in the knowledge that she could do that to him with such ease. It made her feel reckless and bold.

"For a man on the brink of collapse, you seem pretty sturdy to me, *signore*."

"Mmm," he said again, and kissed her, his mouth sleep-warm and sweet against hers.

Fallon gave herself up to the kiss. Then she sighed and buried her face against his shoulder.

"It's going to rain," she said softly.

Stefano groaned. "Just what I need. An impossible weather report in the middle of the night."

"I thought it never rains on Sicily this time of year."

"That's why it's impossible."

"Then why do I hear thunder? There's lightning, too. Back home, that means—"

"You heard thunder? And saw lightning?"

"Yes. Can't you?"

He could, now. Hear the muffled roar, see the sudden sizzle of flame that lit the darkness.

Stefano chuckled, tunneled his fingers into Fallon's hair and kissed the tip of her nose.

"It's obvious you aren't Sicilian, sweetheart. If you were, you'd know that isn't a storm heading toward us."

"Of course it is."

"It's the volcano."

"What?" Fallon shot up in bed, automatically clutching the top sheet to her breasts. "You mean, it's erupting?"

"Etna's been erupting for years." Stefano reached for her. "Come back. I need you in my arms."

"But what's that hitting the windows?"

"Ash, mostly. Maybe some small bits of hardened lava."

Fallon gave a little shriek, forgot about blankets and modesty and ran to the window.

"I've never seen a volcano erupt!"

Stefano rolled his eyes and sat up. He had seen it before. Besides, what he really wanted to see right now was Fallon as he made love to her.

She swung toward him, her face lit by a sudden explosion of flame. Her hair was wild; her eyes were bright with excitement.

She looked like a goddess.

"Stefano, don't you want to come and see this? It's incredible!"

Yes, he thought, and felt his heart turn over, oh, yes, it was.

He reached for his discarded trousers, pulled them on, then jerked the blanket from the bed, went to the window and wrapped her in it.

"Oh," she said, blushing, and he laughed when he realized she'd forgotten she was wearing only her skin and thought that he was covering her because of it.

"Oh, indeed," he said.

He swung her into his arms, kissed her and strode toward the door.

"What are you doing? Stefano, where are we going?"

"You can see the fireworks better from the garden."

"Let me get dressed, then. We can't—"

"We can," he said firmly, and silenced her with another kiss.

It was a perfect night for watching the volcano. The sky was shot with stars and their cold white brilliance formed a backdrop for the hot crimson lava.

Stefano sat in a lounge chair hidden in a stand of flowering hedges, settled Fallon in his lap and pulled the blanket over them both. She leaned back against him, oohing and aahing at the light show.

"Look," she said, "oh, isn't it beautiful?"

"Beautiful," he agreed, even though he couldn't think about anything but the feel of Fallon's skin against his, the silken pressure of her breasts in his palms.

But she was right; the sight was spectacular and Etna was being a lady this night, filling the sky with fire, not danger, and after a while he caught Fallon's excitement, shifted her in his arms so that he could press his cheek against hers and watch the show.

After a while, Fallon gave a little hum of distress.

"What's the matter?"

"I just thought...what if Anna wakes up?"

"What if she does?"

"Well, she might come out here. To watch, like we are. And she might see—"

Stefano grinned. "See what? You, naked in my lap?"

"I'm not naked," she said primly, which was stupid, she knew, because she *was* naked under the blanket, and Stefano's hands were on her breasts.

Oh, the feel of his hands. The faint abrasion of his thumbs, the stroke of his fingertips...

"Where do you live in New York?"

"On Greene Street, in Soho."

"Lots of traffic in Soho."

"So?" She giggled at the unintended pun. "I mean, so what?"

Stefano bit lightly at her neck. "So, I'll bet the traffic doesn't wake you."

"Well, no. But—"

"It's the same thing. The volcano is part of life here. Anna's probably still snoring."

"What about Luigi?"

"What about him? He has an apartment above the garage and the only thing he's ever said about the volcano is that it's a pain in the...behind."

"Well, how about the security—"

Stefano said something in Sicilian, kissed Fallon to silence and told her the only person she had to worry about was him because the feel of her naked bottom shifting as she gestured toward the house and garage was having a predictable effect.

She went still in his arms. He was right. She could feel the ridge of his erection pressing against her.

Suddenly, the fire in the sky was nothing compared to the fire pooling low in her belly.

What had happened tonight had been beyond her wildest dreams. She hadn't planned on letting it happen but once Stefano had kissed her, had told her he wanted her, she couldn't have turned back for anything in the world.

And she wanted him again.

Slowly, deliberately, she turned in his arms until she was facing him. Her lashes dropped over her eyes; she parted her lips and licked them.

"What predictable effect, *signore?*" she murmured.

Stefano growled her name, cupped her face in his hands and took her mouth in a kiss so hot and hungry she moaned.

"You're a witch," he said huskily. "A beautiful, seductive witch."

She kissed him again, snaked the tip of her tongue into his mouth.

"You're playing with fire, *cara.*"

She knew she was, but what was the point in playing it safe? She wanted this moment, this man, wanted him now, here, while the sky burned with fire, and she put her mouth to his ear, bit the lobe...

Stefano shuddered, reached between them, told her what he was going to do to her in explicit language even as he freed himself and surged into her. Fallon cried out and flung her head back, rode him, drove them both higher and higher until their mutual release was as hot as the lava flowing down the mountain.

"Stefano," she sobbed as she collapsed against him, "I've never...it's never been like this before. Never, never..."

He held her, rocked her, stroked her and kissed her as she trembled in his arms. After a while, she quieted; she sighed and drifted into sleep. Still he sat holding her, his face turned to the volcano, and knew that its fiery display was far less powerful than the truth that scorched his heart, his mind, his soul.

He was in love with Fallon.

CHAPTER NINE

FALLON lay on a rattan recliner beside the pool, protected from the sun by a beach umbrella as she basked in the afternoon heat.

She had on a floppy-brimmed hat, sunglasses, a thong bikini and what felt like a ton of sunscreen. Bees buzzed softly in the flowering shrubs that shielded the pool from the house. The sound suited her drowsy mood.

Sighing, she opened one eye, looked up at the sun and decided it was time to turn onto her belly. It was probably the most work she'd done in the couple of hours since she'd come outside and left Stefano to catch up with work in his study, maybe even the most she'd done since they'd become lovers two weeks ago.

Stefano definitely spoiled her.

"I can do that," she'd told him a while ago when he knelt beside her and smoothed sunscreen lotion over her skin.

"I'll do it, *cara*. You know what the doctor said about the dangers of too much sun."

She'd made a face and rolled her eyes and protested that, honestly, he didn't have to fuss over her all the time.

What a lie!

The truth was, she loved having him fuss over her. There was something wonderful in your lover treating you as if you were precious to him.

No man had ever given her that feeling before.

Her lovers had given her expensive gifts, taken her to

clubs where lesser mortals waited behind velvet ropes, showed her off like a glittering trophy.

Stefano had given her flowers, taken her into the privacy of his home, and showed her off to nobody. Their relationship was private and meant for no eyes but their own.

"You're so good to me," she'd murmured as he stroked the lotion over her skin.

His hands had stilled. He turned her over and when she looked into his face, she saw that tight, almost predatory expression on it that she knew meant he wanted her.

"Stefano," she'd murmured, lifting her arms to him, and they'd made love while the breeze sighed and the bees hummed and the water lapped softly against the edge of the pool.

"I'll never have enough of you," he'd whispered afterward, as he lay with his face buried in her throat.

Her arms had tightened around him. She would never have enough of him, either, she'd thought, and struggled not to let the enormity of what she felt for Stefano Lucchesi spill from her lips.

She loved him. Loved him desperately, passionately, in all the June-moon, love-and-marriage ways she'd scoffed at. She'd known it for days. For weeks. And denied it, because the realization was so terrifying.

What if he didn't love her?

She tried not to think about it. She was on a hiatus from reality. So was he. He'd told her as much, lying here with her in his arms a while ago.

He'd made a joke of it, laughed and said his people were half-convinced he'd lost his mind because he'd never stayed away from his office anywhere near this long before.

Then his eyes had become dark.

"Sooner or later, *cara*," he'd said, "we'll both have to go back to the real world."

Fallon felt a coldness creep over her despite the heat

of the Sicilian sun. She knew he was telling her that they'd cocooned themselves in a fantasy world.

He was right. She couldn't expect him to stay here forever. And she couldn't go on hiding much longer, either. The night of the accident, Stefano had phoned the inn where the photo crew was staying. He'd left a message with the manager in Fallon's name, simply saying she'd decided to tack on some vacation time and wouldn't be heading home with them.

Fallon smiled.

Even then, he'd been protective of her.

Once she'd left the hospital, she'd called her mother, told her she'd decided to take a few weeks' vacation. Mary Elizabeth bought the story but when she tried the same ruse on her agent, things hadn't gone as well. Jackie was a New Yorker, born and bred; smokescreens never stopped her.

"Bull," Jackie told her bluntly. "You don't do long vacations, O'Connell, and we both know it. What's going on?"

Nothing, Fallon had insisted. She was tired, that was all, and she needed a rest. After a while, Jackie said yeah, okay, when she was ready to tell her what was going on, she'd be ready to listen.

Fallon rolled onto her belly and rested her face on her arms.

Lying to Jackie had been an act of plain cowardice. It wasn't as if she was playing for time until her face healed enough for her to face the camera again. She'd *never* let herself be photographed again. Her scars would fade a little more with time but basically, what she saw in the mirror now was as good as it was going to get.

Modeling, Jackie, that whole life were already history.

But she wasn't ready to deal with peoples' reactions to her. Her mother's anguish. Her siblings' sympathy. The thinly veiled looks of horror from her business associates, the blood-in-the-water feeding frenzy of the tabloids.

She was safe from all of that here. And happy. Happier than she'd ever been in her life, despite the accident. She'd never known such peace and joy as she'd found in this quiet place with a man who'd been a stranger less than a month ago.

Now she understood what she'd seen in her brother's face the day of his wedding. Keir had stripped his soul bare for Cassie. That was what being in love was all about. Your lover could show you heaven with a kiss or send you to hell with a careless word. She'd never been in love but she'd seen what happened to others.

Crossing Fifty-seventh Street wearing a blindfold back home was less dangerous than falling in love.

She was careful not to say "I love you" to Stefano, though the words were always on her lips.

Maybe he'd say them first.

Maybe she'd awaken one morning in his arms and he'd tell her what she yearned to hear, that he adored her, wanted her, needed her...

"Hey."

Stefano's soft voice and warm breath were at her ear. Fallon turned over and smiled.

"Hey yourself." She snaked her arms around his neck and brought his mouth to hers. "Did you get a lot of work finished?"

"Uh-huh." Stefano sat down on the edge of the lounger and gathered her into his arms. He'd changed into a swimsuit and his skin carried the coolness of the high-ceilinged rooms inside the *castello*. "And you? Did you get a lot of resting done?"

Fallon grinned. "Any more resting and I'll turn into a sloth and start hanging, upside down, from the branches of the nearest tree." She ran her hands over his muscled chest. "Mmm. My own personal air conditioner. Very nice."

"I'm glad you approve." Smiling, he ran his hands

down her arms. "You're as toasty as a fire on a winter afternoon."

"Sicilian sun will do it, every time."

"You smell delicious, too," he said, nuzzling her hair aside and kissing her throat. "What are you wearing?"

Fallon batted her lashes. "An exclusive fragrance, *signore. Eau de Sunscreen.*"

"Eau de Woman," Stefano said, laughing as he kissed her mouth again. His hands skimmed over her back, around her ribs and cupped her breasts. "You should take this suit off, *cara,* and get an all-over tan."

Fallon caught her breath as he rubbed his thumbs over her nipples.

"An all-over tan, huh?"

"Yes." Stefano reached behind her and undid the bra's clasp. "All in the interests of good health, of course."

"Of course. Your suggestion couldn't possibly have anything to do with—" her breath caught as he bent and kissed her naked flesh "—with getting me out of my clothes."

His laugh was low and incredibly sexy. "And it worked."

"Brilliantly," Fallon whispered as she lifted her hips so he could slip off the tiny thong that covered her. "Your turn," she said, and cupped the hardness of his arousal.

Seconds later, they were both naked and Stefano was deep inside her, and the scents and sighs of their love-making drifted languidly on the warm, sea-scented air.

Afterward, sated, they lay quietly in each other's arms.

"We should go in," Fallon said lazily.

"Mmm." Stefano gathered her closer. "Soon."

"I have to shower."

"Mmm."

She sighed, closed her eyes and snuggled against him. "Want to go for a walk on the beach?"

Stefano ran his hand up and down her back in long, soothing strokes.

"Too much effort."

She smiled, her lips curving against his throat. "How about me beating you at Scrabble again?"

"You only beat me because you refuse to let me use perfectly acceptable words."

"'Qat' and 'zuz' are not words, acceptable or otherwise."

Stefano laughed, rolled onto his back and drew her on top of him.

"You're just ticked off because I took you to the cleaners playing poker last night."

"The least you could have done was told me that was how you'd made your first stake," Fallon said, trying to sound indignant and failing. It was difficult to sound indignant when you were pressed, naked, against your lover's sexy body and his hands were gently cupping your bottom.

"I did tell you."

"Uh-huh. After I'd lost the game. You took advantage of me, Lucchesi."

Stefano worked at looking wounded. "How about some credit here? We could have been playing strip poker."

"As if I'd have agreed to that," Fallon said haughtily, and spoiled the act by nipping at his bottom lip. "Actually, that sounds like fun."

"Only because you owe me a hundred trillion *lire*."

They both grinned. Stefano thought, as he did a dozen times each day, how happy it made him to see her smile. Would she still be smiling after he told her what he had in mind?

"Actually," he said, clearing his throat, "I thought we'd try something different this evening."

Fallon folded her arms on his chest. "Strip Scrabble?"

He smiled, took a strand of her hair and wrapped it around his finger.

"That's tempting, *cara,* but I thought we'd drive into Catania for an early supper."

She became stiff in his arms. "What for?"

"I told you," he said patiently, "for an early supper. And I thought you might like to see the shops. There are some little galleries near the harbor—"

"I'm not in the mood for shopping."

"In that case, we'll just go in for supper. I made reservations at a little café on the water—"

"No, thank you."

Fallon tried to roll away from him. Stefano expected it and tightened his arms around her.

"Don't turn away from me, *cara.*"

"I'm getting up, that's all. The sun—"

"The café won't be crowded early on a weekday evening."

"How nice," she said politely.

"A quiet meal, some wine—"

"I said no."

"Fallon." He tilted her face to his. "You have to face the world sometime."

"And what a wonderful way of putting it that is."

Her tone was bitter but he wasn't going to let himself be drawn into an argument, not when he'd just spent an hour making calls to New York, dragging his top people out of late dinners and early beds, trying his damnedest to deal with a problem without flying back and handling it in person.

His attempts had been useless. He had to go back, and there wasn't a way in hell he'd do that before he settled things here.

"You can do this," he said softly. "And you won't be alone. I'll be with you."

She swung her legs off the recliner and this time, he let her go. She rose, grabbed an oversize towel from the table beside them and wrapped it around her body.

"I'm not going with you. I can't make it any clearer than that."

"You *are* going. I can't make it any clearer than that."

Her eyes flashed. "I don't take orders from you or anybody else."

Stefano sat up, reached for a towel and wrapped it around his hips. Hell, what a mess he was making of things.

"Let's start again," he said carefully. "I don't want to quarrel over this."

Fallon nodded. "No." Her voice was very low; he had to strain to hear it. "Neither do I."

"Good." He forced a smile to his lips as he stood up and cupped her shoulders. "*Cara.* Come to Catania and have supper with me. I know a little restaurant I'm sure you'll like."

"I'm sure I would, too," she said, her smile as false as his, "but I don't feel like having dinner out. *You* go. I'll have supper here."

Stefano glared at her. So much for trying again. He'd forgotten that she could be as stubborn as she was beautiful.

"Don't be ridiculous."

"I'm being practical. You must be going stir-crazy, never going anywhere, never seeing anyone, never doing anything except—"

"This isn't about me going out and you know it."

Fallon flashed a bright smile. "Really, I won't mind. A host doesn't have to feel housebound just because his guest—"

He cursed, not in Sicilian but in English as pithy as only a man raised in New York could. His fingers bit into her shoulders.

"That's crap. You're not my guest."

"All right. Maybe that's a little formal."

"And I'm sure as hell not your host. I'm the man who—"

Who what? He stared at her blankly. This was hardly the time to tell her he loved her. Declarations of love deserved the softness of moonlight and the scent of roses, not a sun hot enough to be lethal and the smell of chlorine.

Besides, he'd promised himself not to say anything until he was sure she was ready to hear it. In a handful of weeks, Fallon had dealt with a horrendous accident that had changed her life. He wanted to give her time to be whole again.

And he didn't want her to confuse her feelings for him with gratitude.

Now, he'd almost ruined everything, almost blurted out the most important message of his life with no finesse, no planning, no—

"The man who—?" she said softly. "Who what?"

He felt a muscle jump in his jaw. "Who can't imagine going anywhere without you. Come with me, sweetheart. It'll be all right, I promise."

It was the closest he'd come to saying he loved her. How could she turn him down? Fallon took a deep breath and went into his arms.

Once again, Stefano waited on the terrace. Once again, he paced it from end to end.

He'd paced his own bedroom, too, the one he now shared with Fallon, and the sitting room attached to it, staring at the bathroom door each time he walked by, wondering what she could be doing in there that could take so long and telling himself that it was none of his business.

He knew women. They had little rites of passage they followed before going out in public. Face, hair, nails. He didn't mind that. He was just afraid Fallon was frozen before the mirror, trying to hide a face that didn't need hiding.

He thought about knocking on the door and telling her

that. Then he thought better of it and that was when he headed downstairs to the terrace.

"Stefano?"

He swung around and saw the most beautiful woman in the world step through the door.

Fallon was wearing a short dress in some kind of gauzy material. It had little straps and a short skirt that showed off her legs. She'd pulled her hair back from the unscarred side of her face and let the rest of it dip over her temple and cheek in a delicate fall that softened the scars without hiding them.

It was a brave thing, a wonderful thing, and he felt a rush of love so fierce it terrified him. Thinking you were in love was one thing; knowing it, giving away your heart, was another and he knew, in that moment, that was exactly what he'd done.

What would the world think of *il lupo solo* now? he wondered, and the thought made him smile.

"Do I look all right?" Fallon lifted her hand to her hair, danced her fingers over the glossy black wing that kissed her cheek. "I figured, if we're going to do this, we might as well do it right."

"You look beautiful, *cara*," he said, going to her and drawing her into his arms. "More beautiful than you can possibly know." He kissed her, a long, tender kiss that deepened as she rested her hands on his chest and responded to it. "Just keep that thought," he whispered. "Okay? *We're* doing this. Together."

She smiled as he took her hand in his.

"I'm scared silly," she said. "I couldn't do this without you."

He grinned and kissed her again. "I don't want you doing anything without me," he said, and he put his arm around her waist and walked her to the car.

Stefano was right.

There were some wonderful shops near the harbor.

Fallon dragged him into half a dozen of them, oohing and aahing over everything she saw.

She was self-conscious at first but after a while, she lost herself in the fun of the shopping expedition and she forgot to wonder whether anyone was staring at her or, worse still, looking at her with pity in their eyes.

"I have to buy presents for my family," she told Stefano. He knew their names by now and a little bit about them, and he trooped after her good-naturedly as she selected beribboned tambourines for Meg and Bree, good luck charms carved from lava for Cullen and Sean, and a beautiful terra-cotta bowl for her mother and stepfather.

Fallon paused in the last shop. Something caught her eye. It was the figure of a knight, dressed in armor. Was it a puppet?

"Those are marionettes, *signorina*," the salesclerk said, leaning in and following her gaze. "All made by hand. Marionettes date far back in the history of the Sicilian people. Would you like to see them?"

Only one, Fallon thought, and looked at Stefano. He was leaning against a counter, arms filled with packages, ankles crossed, wearing the polite smile and glazed look of a man who'd long ago tuned out.

"Stefano." She touched his chest and he blinked and smiled into her eyes, and she thought, as she had thought a hundred times in the past hour, how much she adored him...

And how much she'd hoped that what he'd been going to say, this afternoon, was that he was the man who loved her.

"Yes, *cara*. Do you see something you like?"

"Why don't you wait for me outside? I know it's crowded in here."

He glanced at the door and the street like a man granted a reprieve.

"No," he said valiantly, "I'm fine."

"And so am I," she said softly. "I am. Really. I can do this myself."

He bent his head and gave her a long, sweet kiss. The salesclerk cleared her throat; Fallon blushed and Stefano grinned, then sauntered out the door. As soon as he was gone, Fallon pointed to the marionette dressed in a knight's regalia.

"That one," she said, and had it gift-wrapped for her very own knight, who had taken her to live in his castle.

The little café was as charming as Stefano had promised.

They sat at a table overlooking the water. Fallon took one look at the menu and gave up.

"You order," she told Stefano.

Their meal was delicious; the wine warm and strong.

"It's a little rough," Stefano said, "but it's local."

"It's real," Fallon said. "That's good. Things that are real are what matter most."

Stefano reached for her hand and brought it to his lips.

"You're an incredible woman," he said softly.

She shook her head. "I've taken all my strength from you. I'm glad you didn't let me stay home and feel sorry for myself."

"*Cara.* I didn't mean—"

He felt her hand tighten in his. Her face had paled and at the same moment he realized she'd forgotten about her scars, that she'd somehow pushed her hair back behind her ear, he realized she was staring past him.

He looked around, ready to take on the world…and saw a man and woman seated at the next table with a little girl, four or five years old. The child was staring at Fallon, her eyes rounded with fascination; the father had hold of her arm and was talking to her in a low, urgent whisper.

No, Stefano thought, *please, no…*

Too late.

"Mommy," the kid said in perfect American English, "Daddy, what happened to that lady's face?"

The woman paled. The man compressed his lips into an angry line.

"Hush," he said sharply.

Stefano's hand tightened on Fallon's and almost crushed it, but she reached down into a part of herself she hadn't known existed, took a deep breath and said, in a voice that carried as clearly as a bell, that it was all right, children were naturally honest.

"I had an accident," she added. Her eyes met Stefano's. "But I'm all better now."

Stefano dropped a handful of bills on the table. He put his arm around Fallon as they left the café and walked slowly through the warm night to his car. She wasn't quite as unaffected by what had happened as she'd seemed; he could feel her trembling.

"You were wonderful," he said softly.

She gave a tremulous laugh. "She was just a child. I didn't want her to be frightened."

They reached the car. Stefano had driven it himself; he closed the door after Fallon, got behind the wheel and reached for her hand.

"I repeat," he said softly, "you're an amazing woman, Fallon O'Connell."

Her heart was still thumping. Facing the little girl and everyone else in the café had been hard, but she was happy she'd done it.

She knew she couldn't have, without Stefano.

"You're pretty amazing yourself," she said with a little smile. She thought of the marionette and her smile broadened. "My knight in shining armor."

Stefano gathered her into his arms. "I'm no knight, *cara,* I'm only a man." He hesitated. "And, like any man, I've been avoiding telling you something unpleasant."

Her smile tilted. "What is it?"

He lifted her chin and brushed his lips over hers.

"I spent most of the morning on the phone with New York."

"And?"

"And, an important deal's gone sour. I'd hoped to work things out but—"

Fallon worked at holding her smile. "But, you have to fly back."

"Yes. There's no way around it. I wish there were."

She nodded. "I understand."

Stefano linked his hands in the small of her back. "I'd much rather stay here than go to New York. You know that."

She nodded again, wondering how long he'd be gone, imagining herself walking the beach like an old-time sea captain's wife, staring out to sea while she waited for her man to return.

It didn't sound appealing. She didn't want to be without Stefano, and she couldn't really see herself with nothing to do but wile away time until he returned.

"I'll count the days until—"

"No," he said softly.

"No?" she repeated, uncertainty in her voice.

"You can't wait here for me." Stefano took a breath, then expelled it. "I won't be able to get back to Sicily for months."

Fallon stared at him. People said your life flashed before your eyes when you were drowning, but it wasn't true. She was drowning now and all she could think of was that she had to get through these next moments without losing whatever remained of her pride.

"Oh. Well. Well…" She put her hands on his chest. "Well, I think—I think you misunderstood me. I meant— I meant, of course I'll miss you but we'll see each other again sometime, and—"

"*Cara*. Are you crazy?" His voice was gruff. "Why do you make everything so damned complicated?" He kissed her, hard, and when she tried to jerk her face away, he wouldn't let her. "Did you really think these few weeks together would be enough? I want you to come to

New York with me." He took a deep breath. "Stop looking at me as if you don't understand what I'm saying, *cara.* I want you to live with me and share my life." His eyes darkened. "If that isn't what you want, too, tell me now."

What could she tell him that wouldn't lay her soul bare? Fallon made a sound that was half laugh, half sob, lifted her face to Stefano's and kissed him. With a growl, he took control of the kiss, taking it deep, putting his hands on her with an urgency that set her on fire. She made a little sound of surrender; he nipped at her lip and soothed the tiny wound with his tongue. She whimpered when he broke the kiss and leaned his forehead against hers.

"Another minute," he said with rough urgency, "and I'll take you right here."

His words, the images they conjured, made her breath catch. She whispered his name and lay her hand against him, shuddering at the powerful surge of his erection.

Stefano growled a word in Sicilian, curled his fingers around the nape of her neck and kissed her again. Then he took her hand, enclosed it in his around the gearshift lever, took her back to the *castello,* to his bed, to the world they had created together, and to a passion so intense it threatened to consume them both.

CHAPTER TEN

SOMETHING changed between them that night.

Their lovemaking, always passionate, took on added intensity. Their need for each other was insatiable.

They had to get up early, Stefano said; he'd arranged for his jet to be ready by 8:00 a.m. But they were on fire for each other and even when they drowsed off, Fallon lay close in Stefano's arms, their bodies still joined.

She awoke, again and again, to the incredible feel of his hands and mouth urging her to join in a celebration of their ardor.

"Is it too much for you, *cara?*" he whispered to her once, when she caught her breath.

"Never," she whispered back, "oh, never."

It was true. She couldn't get enough of him. She wanted his touch, his taste, his hard body demanding her compliance. The way he held her as they slept, his arm curved over her waist, his hand cupping her breast, were gestures of pure male possessiveness.

She belonged to him. And that was how she wanted it.

The realization amazed her. She'd never wanted to be owned by anybody. Watching her parents' relationship, the way her mother had always subjugated her needs to her father's, had been a bitter lesson.

But when Stefano held her to him, even as they slept, when he kissed her mouth, her breasts, the very heart of her femininity and whispered that she was his, she felt ecstasy, not fear.

He belonged to her in that same way.

It was why she told him to lie back, why she kissed his throat, his chest, his belly. It was the reason she took him in her mouth during that long night and thrilled to his groans of passion.

She'd never done this with another man, but Stefano was hers, she was his, and she wanted to become one with him as he had become one with her.

At dawn, warm and boneless as a cat, she lay quietly in his arms, her head on his shoulder.

"Do you realize I don't know anything about you?"

Stefano gave a soft, wicked chuckle that made her smile.

"You know what I mean."

He took her hand and brought it to his mouth. "What would you like to know?"

"Well, tell me about the *castello*. What happened to the old castle? Why did you build a new one?"

"It's a long, boring story."

Fallon rolled onto her belly, crossed her arms on his chest and propped her chin on her wrists.

"Tell me."

He stroked her hair, took her back through the centuries and described the pirates, warriors and rebels who'd tried to conquer this land. He told her about his grandfather and the promise he'd made to recover what the old man had lost.

"How did he lose it?"

Stefano smiled. "It's like the plot of a bad opera."

His grandfather's and grandmother's families were old enemies, their troubles going so far back that nobody was sure of the reasons. Somehow, his grandparents met and fell in love anyway. They eloped, and the long-simmering feud burst into flames. People had accidents, disappeared... Eventually, his grandfather decided the only way to protect his wife and children was to abandon his land and start over in America.

"Did he ever regret that decision?"

"Never. A man does what he must for love."

It was a romantic reply but then, the story was wonderfully romantic. Snuggling closer, Fallon asked Stefano to tell her more about himself.

To please her, he talked about things he'd never mentioned to anyone else. The loss of his parents. The initial shock of living with his grandparents. That first stroke of financial luck.

Genius, she said, not luck.

"Or maybe stupidity," he said, laughing, "I could have lost every dollar I'd won."

"But you didn't."

"No. I struck it rich." He rolled her beneath him. "Like I did when I found you."

She smiled. "Flattery will get you everywhere," she said in a teasing whisper.

Stefano gave her a deep, lingering kiss. "You realize," he said softly, "you've ruined my image."

Fallon looked up at him and stroked the dark hair back from his forehead.

"What image?"

"One of the tabloids dubbed me *Il lupo solo*. The lone wolf."

"Mmm." Fallon wound her arms around his neck. "Nice. I've always thought it would be exciting to pet a wolf."

That made him smile. "I'm glad to hear it."

"Why do they call you that?"

"Oh, it started when I was foolish enough to give an interview. The reporter began asking personal questions. I refused to answer them." His tone hardened. "I have a public persona because it's required of me, but my private life isn't for public scrutiny."

"I know how you feel. I've never had a private life. Well, not once I began modeling…"

"Don't," Stefano said quickly. "Please, don't think about the past. The future is what matters."

She nodded and closed her eyes as he began to kiss her. She *was* thinking about the future, but why tell him that? He'd have enough to deal with, now that they were going home. She knew she'd draw attention.

People would talk about her. Her scars didn't matter, Stefano said, but in Sicily, their world had excluded everyone but themselves.

It would be different in New York.

She thought of what had happened in the café. The child had been direct. People back home wouldn't be. They'd smile to her face and whisper behind her back.

"Cara."

Fallon opened her eyes and saw the consternation in Stefano's face. He ran his hand down her body, his touch as protective as it was tender.

"I'll be with you. I'll look after you."

"I know you will, but..." Fallon framed his face with her hands. "They'll be all over you, Stefano. The press, I mean. A man who values his privacy won't enjoy having cameras and microphones shoved in his face."

He smiled, but she could see the steely resolve in the set of his jaw.

"Don't worry about me. I can take care of myself."

She nodded, but she wasn't convinced. For the first time since he'd asked her to live with him when they reached New York, she wondered if she'd agreed too quickly. The tabloids would be drawn to her, not to him. If she moved back into her own apartment, if they saw each other on the quiet...

"Forget that," Stefano growled. "I'm not letting you go."

He saw the surprised look on her face, but reading her mind had been easy. She was afraid of what she'd face back home and wondering if she could avoid attention by staying under the radar.

He wasn't going to let her do that.

He needed her, wanted her in his life, and that realization still stunned him. He'd never needed anyone before. Now, knowing what it was like to be with her, he wasn't going to let Fallon slip away from him.

He'd never understood people who thrived on gossip but he knew damned well there were those who did. That anyone would be interested in telling stories about him always amazed him.

He could only imagine the dirty thrill the jackals would have in talking about Fallon.

Stefano tightened his arms around her.

He'd take care of everything. A couple of calls from his attorneys, the all-too-real threat of an expensive lawsuit, and the sleaze purveyors would back off.

Besides, he'd be with Fallon all the time.

She had nothing to fear.

He would protect her, he promised himself, and then he kissed her, and touched her, and he forgot everything but his growing love for the woman in his arms.

Stefano said he had an apartment on Fifth Avenue.

Fallon laughed when she saw it. Calling a four bedroom, six bathroom duplex with two fireplaces, a sauna and a wraparound terrace overlooking Central Park an "apartment" was like calling the *castello* a cottage.

It was beautiful, she told him, just beautiful.

"You think?" he said, in a way that suggested he'd been wary of her reaction.

"I know! It's incredible. And the view..."

"Yeah." His grin reminded her of a kid on Christmas morning. "That's the real reason I bought the place." He tossed his keys on a small table near the door. "I had a decorator do the rooms but, I don't know, sometimes I think it still needs something."

Fallon was miles ahead of him. Fresh flowers. Some small paintings—the ones she'd found in a French antique shop, for instance—above that couch. Her Chinese rug centered on the marble floor, and those masks she'd picked up in Bali on that wall.

"I have—" She cleared her throat. Funny. She'd been sleeping with this man for weeks; she knew every inch of his body just as he knew every inch of hers, yet suggesting bringing some of her things here and adding them to his seemed almost too personal. "I have some—some stuff," she said, trying to sound casual. "Things I collected in places I've been, and I thought…"

Thought what? Stefano was looking at her so strangely. Maybe she'd gone too far.

"You thought?" he said politely.

"Never mind. It was a silly idea. I mean, this place is so perfect…"

"Tell me what you thought," he said, gathering her into his arms.

"Well…" She played with his tie. "I thought you might like to see how some of my things looked—"

"Here?"

She nodded. Stefano tilted her face up and kissed her. "They'll look wonderful."

"But you haven't even seen them."

"I don't have to. Give up your own place. Move all your things here. You don't need an apartment of your own anymore."

She longed to do it, but logic held her back. Had he really thought about how different life was going to be in New York?

"Let's take things one step at a time," she said carefully. "I mean… This isn't Sicily, Stefano. We had our own world then. Just you and me, and nobody else."

He silenced her with a kiss. "It's still just us. Nobody else matters."

"You've spent your life running from the press, Stefano. I've spent mine dealing with it. They're going to be merciless. They'll want to invade my privacy. *Your* privacy."

"I'll take care of the press," he said grimly.

Fallon touched the tip of her tongue to her top lip. "Maybe. But even if you do, people will talk. They'll have questions."

"Mr. Lucchesi?"

It was Stefano's housekeeper. She'd been good at disguising her reaction to Fallon's scars, but Fallon had seen the quick flash of recognition, then shock followed by a look of pity in the woman's eyes.

"Sir, Miss Allen is here."

A woman came briskly across the marble floor toward them.

"Stefano. I'm sorry to bother you so soon after your arrival, but—" Her voice faltered as she looked at Fallon. There it was again. Recognition. Shock. Pity, intermingled in a way that made Fallon's belly knot. "But some documents came in and they're urgent."

Stefano nodded and introduced Fallon to his PA, but the papers had distracted him and Fallon knew he'd missed the woman's reaction.

"You're going to be busy, Stefano," Fallon said politely. "Why don't I wait on the terrace?"

"Don't go." Stefano glanced up, slid his arm around her waist and drew her against him. "I'll only be a minute." He kissed her lightly and walked a few feet away.

Fallon thought his assistant's eyebrows would fly off her face.

"Um, don't I... Have we met before, Miss O'Connell?"

"You might have seen my picture," Fallon said calmly. "I am—I was—a model."

"Oh. Oh, of course. I knew... I mean, I recognized..."

They stared at each other in strained silence. *Yes,* Fallon wanted to say, *it's me. And yes, my face was cut. And yes, your boss wants me anyway...*

But she said nothing and, after a moment, Stefano rejoined them.

"Well," the PA said briskly, "if you don't need me, sir... Oh. One other thing. You have that Animal Defense Fund dinner tonight."

Stefano glanced at Fallon. "Phone and make my apologies."

"But they're honoring you with—"

"Tell them I'm sorry but something's come up."

"No." Fallon spoke quietly, her words meant only for Stefano. "Please, don't cancel on my account."

"It's your first night home," he said softly. "I'm not going to leave you."

"But the dinner. The award—"

"They'll muddle through without me," he said, and smiled.

Fallon took a deep breath. When she was seven and Meg and Bree, Cullen, Sean and Keir could all swim like seals, she was still afraid to do more than dip one foot in the water. Her mother said she'd had a scare when she was little, something about wading into a lake and everybody thinking somebody else was watching her, and how she'd stepped into deep water, gone under and almost drowned.

"You'll get over the fear," Mary Elizabeth had said gently.

Fallon had. She'd done it by closing her eyes, holding her nose and jumping into the deep end of the pool at the chintzy motel where they'd been living.

Yes, she'd swallowed half the pool and yes, she might have drowned, but she hadn't. She'd survived, learned to swim, and learned a hard lesson.

When you were afraid, the best cure was to shut your eyes, hold your breath and jump.

"I'll go with you," she told Stefano.

"It isn't necessary. One step at a time, remember?"

"I want to go with you," Fallon said, and when she saw how his eyes lit with pleasure, she almost believed that she'd meant it.

After all, people were civilized. She could handle stares and Stefano could handle the rest. How bad could it be?

Bad.

Horrible, to put it bluntly.

Less than a month later, Sicily had receded so far into the distance that it might have been a dream.

To Fallon's surprise, reporters weren't the problem she'd anticipated. Word got out; they came around, but never more than once. She was certain Stefano had done something to keep them at bay. Only a couple of lines hit the gossip columns and, just to be on the safe side, she phoned her mother and told her she'd been in an accident, in case the news spread.

Mary was upset and wanted to fly to New York. Fallon lied, said her injuries were nothing much and promised to come home for a visit over Labor Day weekend. As luck would have it, the rest of her family were out of the country, on business or on vacation, so she didn't have to worry about fooling them.

On the surface, they seemed to have weathered the storm. They hadn't. The problem wasn't publicity.

It was Stefano, and what she was beginning to see in his eyes.

Not shock, of course. He was used to her scars.

What she saw was pity. That same gut-wrenching pity she saw in the eyes of others.

Her lover had a busy public life. A king might want privacy, but kingdoms weren't ruled from the shadows. The city slumbered in end-of-summer heat, which meant that life had moved east to the Hamptons.

Benefits, charity auctions, dinner parties. Invitations poured in and each time he received one, Stefano would tell her about it and say, with an air of studied casualness, *Do you want to go, sweetheart?* And she'd think "no" and say "yes," because she was determined not to change the way he lived.

Fallon had grown accustomed to the changes to her face and years of applying makeup had paid off. She could cover the scars so that they didn't show very much, at least from a distance.

Up close, things were different.

They'd go to whatever function it was and Stefano would hold her hand and introduce her to everyone in a way that made her importance to him clear.

People always said it was nice to meet her and wasn't the weather hot and humid, and all the while she'd see the usual sequence of shocked recognition, horror and pity on their faces and always, *always*, she knew they were trying to figure out why Stefano would have burdened himself with a woman who looked like her.

And then she'd look at Stefano and know *he* knew what she was thinking, and sometimes he'd murmur, *Shall we leave, sweetheart?* and whenever he did, she'd smile and say *No, of course not, this is fun…*

He pitied her. What else could that darkness in his gaze mean?

A woman wanted many things from her lover. Passion, tenderness, fidelity and yes, compassion, but pity? Never.

The worst of it was, she understood what had happened. In Sicily, her face had been the only reality. Stefano could look past it and see her for the woman she was. In all fairness, she knew that he still could.

But for how long?

The women in Stefano's circle had perfect faces, if not through genes and nature then by the skilled hands of a surgeon.

She heard snatches of female conversation, references to this plastic surgeon or that; once, she walked into a ladies' room and overheard two women in adjoining stalls discussing the miracles performed by a certain doctor. Their voices were loud enough, their comments deliberate enough so she half suspected the information was meant for her.

She did think about seeing a surgeon—someone in the States might have a different technique for dealing with her scars than the doctor in Italy—but she wasn't ready for that. She wanted to get used to this new face, this real face, before she made any decisions about changing it.

God help her, she wanted Stefano to tell her he loved her, and to tell it to her while she still looked like this.

At night, she lay in his arms, knowing he was as wide-awake as she, wondering what he was thinking. She wanted to ask him, but she was afraid to. If she was right and that was pity she saw in his eyes, if he could no longer see beyond her scars...

No. She wouldn't think that way.

Maybe she had too much time on her hands. She'd worked hard all her adult life. She'd never sat around for so long without doing something productive.

One morning, after Stefano left for a meeting, she dressed in a Chanel suit and a pair of Jimmy Choo stiletto heels and went to her agent's office. She'd already spoken to Jackie and told her about the accident, but they had yet to see each other.

It was tough, walking into the agency, striding past the photos of all the perfect faces that adorned the walls—photos that still included hers—and tougher still to see the flash of compassion in Jackie's eyes when Fallon whipped off her oversize dark glasses.

"I need a job," Fallon said bluntly.

Compassion didn't keep Jackie from being blunt.

"I can't use you anymore. Your face—"

"I know everything about this business, Jackie. Surely, somebody can use me for something."

Jackie tossed her pen aside and sat back. "I'm an agent, not an employment office."

"But you know people. You hear things."

Her agent tapped a finger against her lip. "Well, yeah. Matter of fact, I had lunch with Carla Kennedy yesterday. Wasn't your last assignment with her?"

"Does Carla have a job I could handle?"

"She's looking for an assistant." Jackie smiled. "A gopher. Go for this, go for that… You know the drill. Lie to people she doesn't want to deal with when they phone, make barely enough money to pay your bills…" Jackie's grin widened. "Though from what I hear, paying bills isn't your problem. You've got somebody to do that."

Fallon rose to her feet. "Thanks for the tip," she said politely. "And by the way, I haven't 'got' anyone to pay my bills. I made a lot of money, Jackie. You should know that. You got fifteen percent right off the top but what the government didn't take in taxes, I saved."

"I only meant—"

Fallon didn't want to hear the rest. She left the office, made her way through the cramped waiting room packed with hopeful girls from little towns nobody had ever heard of and taxied straight to the offices of *Bridal Dreams* magazine.

She gave her name to the receptionist and didn't flinch when the girl's eyes widened after a glance at her face.

Carla came bustling out to the desk to greet her.

"Sweetie," she said, "oh, you poor baby. I just heard the news the other day… Oh, my God, your poor face! Darling, what are you going to do? Have you seen a plastic surgeon?"

"No," Fallon said briskly. "I heard you're looking for an assistant."

"I can get some names for you. There's this incredible guy who took, I swear, ten years off Irene Whitmore's face—"

"*Are* you looking for an assistant, Carla?"

"Yeah, but why would you care?" Carla's smile seemed to tighten. "I also heard you're having a thing with Stefano Lucchesi. Is it true?"

"I really didn't come here to talk about myself," Fallon said pleasantly. "About that assistant's job…"

"What about it?" Carla blinked. "You mean… You?

You're interested in...?'' Her voice dropped to a purr. "Don't tell me your boyfriend isn't paying your bills, darling. He has scads of money.''

"The job,'' Fallon said coolly. "Is there one or isn't there?''

Carla led Fallon into her crowded office, motioned her to a chair while she perched on the edge of her desk, swinging one long leg over the other.

"It's not a job for a prima donna.''

"I didn't think it was.''

"Three hundred a week,'' Carla said brusquely, "half an hour for lunch, no medical, dental or anything else. Still interested?''

Fallon had earned more than that in ten minutes, but the money didn't matter. Feeling useful—not having endless time to brood and think foolish thoughts—did.

"Yes,'' she said, and held out her hand. Carla ignored it.

"Does your boyfriend know you're going to be working for me?''

"I haven't told him yet.''

Carla seemed to find that amusing. "You're hired,'' she said, and smiled like a cat anticipating a mouse fillet.

Fallon waited a week before telling Stefano.

She had the feeling he wouldn't like her news. She kept thinking back to her second day in Sicily, to Carla taking a call on her cell phone and then staring up at the *castello* as if she'd seen a ghost before taking off in a rush. And there were the lies Carla had told about the owner of the castle.

What was all that about?

Why hadn't she ever asked Stefano?

Something had gone wrong in the deal he'd made with Carla and *Bridal Dreams,* but that was another thing she only now wondered about.

Why would a man who cherished his privacy give permission to a magazine to film on his property?

Things had happened too quickly to ask questions in Sicily, and now they were happening the same way. There was a rift growing between her and Stefano. Not a big one: he still held her through the night and they still made love with that same intensity, but the lazy ease between them had been replaced by an almost cautious politeness.

She waited to tell him about her job until they were spending a rare evening at home.

"Stefano." He looked up from a magazine and Fallon took a deep breath. "I've taken a job."

He gave her a puzzled smile. "A job?"

She nodded. "Yes. Last week."

His smile tilted. "You took a job last week and you're only now telling me?"

A flush rose in her cheeks. He saw it and could have bitten his tongue off but then he thought, no, why shouldn't he be irritated? Fallon was changing; she'd become more quiet, more reserved, and now she'd found a job and never thought to mention it? Was she so unhappy, living here with him?

"I'm working at *Bridal Dreams* magazine as Carla Kennedy's assistant."

He blinked. Surely, he'd heard that wrong. "I beg your pardon?"

"I said—"

"You're working for Carla?"

"Yes."

"Why?"

"Because she needed an assistant and offered me the job. That's why."

"She phoned, out of the clear blue sky, and offered a job to you?"

"No. Of course not."

"You approached her."

"Damn it, why the inquisition? Yes. I approached her."

"And you did this without telling me?"

"Yes."

Stefano tossed aside the magazine. What the hell was going on? Was the woman who'd been content walking the cliffs with him so bored with her new life that she'd gone to work for his former mistress?

It sounded like the setup for a bad joke. The woman he loved, working for the woman he'd slept with and discarded.

But Fallon didn't know that. Carla, on the other hand, was probably laughing her head off.

"Well, you're not going to work for her anymore." He spoke coolly, which surprised him because what he wanted to do was shout. "Call her in the morning and tell her you quit."

"Excuse me?"

"There's no reason for you to work, Fallon. If you need money—"

Her color deepened. "This isn't about money."

"It's my fault," he said, in tones he meant to be conciliatory. "I should have opened an account in your—"

"I do not need money from you, Stefano."

"There's nothing wrong in needing—"

"Damn it, are you deaf?" Fallon shot to her feet. "I'm perfectly capable of supporting myself."

"Then why did you take a job with Carla Kennedy?"

"I like to work. I *need* to work."

He nodded, as if he understood, but he didn't. She needed to work? Why? She had him in her life now. She could redecorate this mausoleum of an apartment. She could come to his office and meet him for lunch. She could do anything she wanted, just as long as it included him.

Fallon had changed since Sicily.

She moped, she didn't laugh, she insisted on going to the endless rounds of charity benefits he'd simply sent checks to in the past, and he'd be damned if he knew the reason when all he saw in her eyes once they arrived at a party was sorrow each time some insensitive idiot couldn't keep his eyes off her beautiful, wounded face.

"What am I to you, Stefano?" Fallon said quietly. "Tell me."

His tongue felt glued to the roof of his mouth. My heart, he thought. My beloved. But how could he admit that until she was ready to hear it? Until she accepted herself as she was? Until she was whole?

"You're my responsibility," he said carefully. "I want to take care of you, Fallon. Surely, you know that."

She nodded. It wasn't the answer she'd prayed for, but at least it was honest.

"I do know it. But *you* must know that it's important I begin taking care of myself again."

Damn it, if he wasn't careful he was going to drive her away. Stefano swallowed his bewilderment and his anger. He reached for Fallon and took her in his arms.

"Cara," he said softly. "This is a foolish thing to argue over."

He felt her relax against him. "Yes. It is."

"If you want to work, you should. But not for Carla."

"Why not?"

He took a deep breath. "She's a liar. She's not someone to be trusted."

"How do you know that?"

She was, as always, incisive and persistent. He admired her for that even as he tried to figure out what to say. How did a man tell the woman he loved that he'd had an affair with a woman she knew? A woman she saw every day? He knew Fallon didn't think he'd lived like a monk, but still...

A man broke such news cautiously, that was how. And caution meant not making such an admission to a woman who was already angry at you.

"Carla and I had an agreement for that shoot at the *castello* and she reneged on it."

"I've been meaning to ask you about that. How come you let *Bridal Dreams* take photographs there to begin with?"

Stefano managed a wry smile. "Carla made me an offer I couldn't refuse."

"What offer?"

"Must we discuss this now?" he said impatiently. He slid his hands up her arms, then down again to her wrists. "If you must work, I'd prefer you to find another job. Will you do that?" He smiled and tipped her chin up. "For me?"

Fallon sighed. Stefano had done so much for her. Surely, she could do this for him.

"Will you? Please?"

"Yes. If it's what you want, Stefano, I will."

She leaned against him, loving the feel of him, the strength of him, and all at once she knew that what she really wanted to talk about had nothing to do with Carla.

"Tell me something," she said in a low voice. "How would you feel if—if I saw a plastic surgeon?"

His expression didn't change but it didn't have to. A stillness came over him. He glanced at her scars, his gaze quick and guilty.

"The decision would be yours," he said carefully. "I wouldn't want to influence you."

Fallon nodded. She wanted to weep but she didn't. What should he have said? That he saw past her scars? That what he'd told her in Sicily held true in New York? That he wanted her for who she was, not for who she had been?

Somehow, she forced a smile.

"Thank you," she said, "for being honest."

"I would never lie to you," Stefano said.

It wasn't true and he knew it. He lied each day, by not telling her that he loved her.

He'd lied just now, by not telling her he didn't want her to go under the surgeon's knife.

He'd lied by not telling her about Carla.

I'm contemptible, he thought fiercely. *The only time I don't lie to her is when we make love.*

He crushed her mouth beneath his until she clung to him and moaned his name. Then he carried her into his bedroom, and sought to expiate his guilt by making love to her through the long night.

CHAPTER ELEVEN

THE next morning, Stefano disappeared into his study before breakfast. When he emerged, he said he had to fly out of town but that he'd be back in time for dinner.

"Just us," he said, taking Fallon in his arms. "We'll have a quiet evening. Is that okay with you?"

It was wonderful. She'd have bartered her soul for more like it.

"Yes," she said, "it's very okay."

Stefano leaned his forehead against hers. "I'm sorry I flew off the handle last night. We shouldn't have quarreled."

"It was my fault." Fallon looped her arms around his neck. "I should have told you about my job."

Stefano gathered her against him, holding her close.

"There are things I should tell you, too." He went on holding her, as if he never wanted to let her go. Then he lifted her face to his and kissed her, his mouth gentle and warm against hers. "We need to talk," he said softly.

Fallon nodded. "Tonight."

"Tonight," he echoed.

He kissed her again. There was something in the kiss that frightened her, a kind of finality, but before she could ask him about it, he let go of her, slung his jacket over his shoulder and went out the door.

Fallon stood alone in the marble-floored foyer for a long moment. It was silly, reading meaning into a kiss when what she needed to concentrate on were things that were in her hands.

Quitting her job, for example. Carla wouldn't be happy—she'd turned out to be a short-tempered boss who expected things to be done when she snapped her fingers, and Fallon was in the middle of organizing her files. Well, she'd stay on for a week, if Carla insisted. Stefano was a businessman; he'd surely understand that.

And then—and then there was what she'd decided about surgery. She'd raised the issue, not Stefano, but she'd seen his reaction. Still, she'd come to the conclusion that she wasn't going to do it. Not yet. Not until she was sure she was doing it for herself and not for him.

She loved him—oh, how she wished she felt free to tell him that—but something so drastic had to be for her, not for anyone else.

Fallon drew a deep breath, expelled it, gave herself a last check in the mirror and headed out the door.

The *Bridal Dreams* offices were in total confusion.

Something had gone wrong with distribution in the Midwest, the colors of the current cover were completely off, and the designer Carla intended to feature in the May issue had just revealed she was really a he and was tired of being in the closet.

Carla ran around barking orders and accusing everyone, including the kid who brought lunch from the corner deli, of trying to destroy her.

Under those circumstances, Fallon didn't have the heart to drop the news that she was quitting.

Things quieted down in late afternoon and she stuck her head around the half-open door to Carla's office.

"Carla? Do you have a minute?"

"Barely," Carla said irritably. "I hope you've come to tell me you finished with those files."

"Not yet. It's a major overhaul and—"

"I don't need excuses, Fallon. Just do your job and let me know when you're done."

Fallon shut the door behind her and came into the office. Carla looked up, surprised, as she sat down on the other side of the desk.

"I came to tell you I'm quitting. I'll finish the files," she added quickly, "but you'll have to find someone else."

Carla sat back, her eyes narrowing as they fixed on Fallon.

"I should have expected it. You think you're too good for what you're doing."

"It isn't that."

"Give me a break!" Carla smiled coldly. "You're accustomed to having everyone fussing over you and here you are, squatting in front of a dusty file cabinet or trailing around after me. As I said, I should have known."

"I'm quitting for personal reasons, Carla. They have nothing to do with you."

"What personal reasons?"

"I don't see any need to go into them." Fallon stood up. "I thought it only fair to give you notice. If you need me to stay through the end of next week—"

"It's your boyfriend."

"What?" Fallon felt her cheeks flush. "No. Stefano has nothing to do with—"

"He doesn't like you working for me."

"I told you, he has—"

"You can't lie worth a damn, O'Connell." Carla hunched forward, a thin smile on her face. "What's the problem? Does he think this is beneath you? Is he afraid people might think he isn't supporting you properly?"

"I'm not going to discuss my personal life," Fallon said coldly. She turned and reached for the door. "As I said, if you need me to stay until—"

"Or does he worry that the woman he slept with a couple of months ago and the woman he's sleeping with now are liable to compare notes?"

Fallon felt the blood drain from her head. Her hand

froze on the doorknob. Turn around, she told herself, turn around and face her.

"Men are funny," Carla purred. "Always worried we'll share their little idiosyncrasies. Not that we would, darling. After all, we both know what a fantastic lover Stefano is—though I must admit, I have wondered if he plays the same little games with you as he did with me. Taking your hands, for example. Putting them—"

"Stop it!" Fallon whirled toward the other woman. "Just stop it right now."

"Why? It's the twenty-first century, Fallon. Women are free to talk about sex if they…" She paused, and a knowing smile curved her mouth. "Oh, my," she said softly. "You didn't know. Stefano didn't tell you. Here you are, working as my little gopher, and you had no idea I knew your lover as well as you do. Better, probably, considering all the months he and I were together."

Fallon stared at that cold, lovely face, the hateful smile and the venom-filled eyes. She told herself she was being ridiculous. Stefano wasn't a monk. Of course there'd been women in his life. There'd been men in hers. What did it matter?

Except it did matter. He should have told her. Instead, he'd snapped and snarled and told her lies.

Hadn't it occurred to him that if she found out about Carla—*when* she found out—it would be humiliating to hear the news from anyone but him?

"Do sit down," Carla said pleasantly, "before you pass out."

"Don't be ridiculous!"

"Well, you're white as a sheet. Sit down, darling." Carla laughed. "I know getting coffee is your job, but I'll pour you a cup, if you need it."

Fallon sank into the chair. "I'm fine."

"He really didn't tell you?"

Fallon shook her head. "No."

"Ah." Carla folded her arms and leaned back. "Well,

I suppose we can hardly blame him. I mean, it all happened so quickly, me ending our relationship, him getting involved with you..."

"You ended it?"

"Oh, of course. And Stefano was furious. Well, we'd been together six months. I suppose he assumed... Anyway, women don't walk out on men like him. That's what he thinks, anyway." Carla's voice turned syrupsweet. "Are you sure you want to hear this?"

"I don't care one way or the other," Fallon said, lying through her teeth.

"Well, anyway, it's all water under the bridge." Carla sighed. "I knew he was liable to do something crazy. I mean, when I told him we were finished, he was so upset... Oh, darling. I don't meant to imply that taking up with you was crazy, just that, well, there he was, being vindictive, saying he wouldn't let me use the inside of his castle because I'd hurt him, then phoning me the second day of the shoot to say he was going to find a way to make me change my mind about walking out on him..."

Carla kept talking but Fallon had stopped listening. The phone call. The second day of the shoot. Carla, whitefaced, turning to stare at the *castello,* then offering a sorry excuse and rushing back to New York.

It made terrible sense.

Stefano had taken up with her on the rebound. And he'd taken her to the same bed Carla had slept in.

Fallon lurched to her feet. "I'm sorry, Carla, but I have to leave early."

"I've upset you."

Bitch! That was the whole purpose of the conversation. Did Carla think she'd been born yesterday?

"No," Fallon said, and forced a quick smile, "you haven't." She dug deep and managed to turn the smile into a just-between-us grin. "Men are impossible. Why Stefano would think it would bother me if he told me that you and he had—that you'd been involved, is beyond me.''

"You're right," Carla said blandly. She hesitated, then leaned forward. "Darling? Do you want the name of that surgeon I mentioned? I mean, I'm sure your face isn't a problem for you but, well, knowing Stefano..."

"Yes?" Fallon said coldly. "Knowing him, what?"

"Nothing. It's just that he's such a perfectionist."

"My face isn't a problem for him," Fallon said, even more coldly. "If that's what you're suggesting."

"Perhaps not directly but, um, people talk. Well, no matter. Stefano's shown you such enormous compassion..."

"He has, yes." Fallon stared at the other woman, knowing that the best way to strike at her was to go for the jugular. "Perhaps that's why he never mentioned his relationship with you to me, Carla. I don't think it left much of an impression on him."

She made her exit on that note. It was pathetic, the saddest excuse for victory in the world, but it was all she could manage.

Swiftly, Fallon collected her suit jacket, her purse and headed for the street. Stefano had said he'd be back by early evening. And that they had to talk. Good. She wanted to talk, too.

About relationships.

About integrity.

Fallon stepped off the curb, ignored the traffic whizzing past her toes and, in the time-honored way New Yorkers hailed cabs, lifted her hand. A taxi swung out of traffic, horns blared, and the vehicle stopped beside her.

She climbed in, gave the driver Stefano's address, then tapped her foot all the way there.

Stefano unlocked the front door, dumped his keys and his briefcase on the table.

He called out his housekeeper's name, then remembered it was her day off.

Just as well.

He'd gotten back to the city earlier than expected and really didn't feel like bothering with anyone right now, not even his housekeeper.

What he wanted was to strip off his clothes, take a long, cold shower, put on shorts and a T-shirt, mix a pitcher of Margaritas—Fallon liked Margaritas, he thought, smiling—and put it in the refrigerator to chill while he did some serious thinking before she got home.

Stefano dropped his clothes on a chair in the dressing room.

He'd better do some serious thinking. He'd already made a couple of really bad errors. First and most important, he should have already told Fallon that he loved her. He was as sure as a man dared be that she loved him, too.

If there was any danger in telling her how he felt, he'd be damned if he could see it anymore.

Stefano turned on the shower, stepped inside and let the side and overhead sprays pelt his knotted muscles. He was tired; he hadn't slept much last night, lying in bed thinking about how life could turn things upside down.

How the woman you wanted to spend the rest of your life with could end up working for a woman you never wanted to see again.

Hell.

That had been his second mistake. He should have taken a deep breath, looked Fallon straight in the eye last night and said, *I don't want you working for Carla because I had an affair with her.*

Instead, he'd chickened out. Said nothing. Done nothing. Breathed a sigh of relief that Carla hadn't been the vindictive bitch he'd have figured her for, and kept his mouth shut because he hadn't been able to think of a way to tell Fallon the truth.

He'd had an affair with Carla and ended it because it

was time for it to end. Carla hadn't meant a damned thing to him except, at the end, trouble.

Stefano turned the water off and reached for a towel.

Well, he wasn't going to screw up anymore. As soon as Fallon came through the door, he'd sit her down and tell her everything, starting with the fact that he loved her.

He smiled and wrapped the towel low on his hips, but his smile faded as he thought of the third thing he had to tell Fallon.

It was the reason he'd flown to Boston.

He had a college buddy there, a guy who'd become a physician and headed up a department of one of the country's most prestigious hospitals. Jeff was a cardio-thoracic surgeon. He literally held people's hearts in his hand. He was the best, and Stefano had figured he'd know only the best.

If Fallon wanted restorative surgery on her scars, only the best would do.

"How bad are the scars?" Jeff had asked him.

"Not bad enough for her to go under the knife," he'd answered, and Jeff's eyebrows had risen.

"So it's like that, huh?"

"Like what?"

Jeff had grinned. "Like you finally found the right woman."

Stefano hadn't bothered denying it. "Yes. Damned right I did, and why she wants this surgery is beyond me."

"Does she want it for herself?" Jeff said.

It had been Stefano's turn to raise his eyebrows. "Of course. Who else would she want it for?"

Jeff shrugged. "You, maybe. I mean, if she thinks—"

"I love her just as she is. She knows that. Look, she was a model. I thought she'd gotten past looking in the mirror and only seeing those scars, but I was wrong."

"Yeah, that happens. Okay, my man. I'll give you the names of two guys in New York."

"The best?"

Jeff grinned. "The absolute best. As long as the lady wants this for herself—"

"Of course, I'm going to try and talk her out of it."

"No, you won't."

"Sure I will. She caught me off guard, bringing the subject up last night, but I'm certainly not going to let her undergo surgery if... What?"

"Listen, I understand. You love the lady. You want to take care of her. But this is her face, Stefano, her life and her choice. Be there with her when she goes to see these men, discuss the pros and cons with her if she wants, maybe offer your opinion on which guy to go with if she asks, but don't try talking her into, or out of, anything."

"This is one hell of a major decision, Jeff. I can't just let her—"

"Yeah, pal. You can."

Stefano reached for his discarded trousers, dug into the pockets and took out the slip of paper on which Jeff had written the names and numbers of the surgeons he'd recommended.

Okay. Jeff was the doctor; he was just a man so much in love that he could hardly see straight. He'd play this whatever way Fallon wanted, and—

The front door opened, then slammed shut.

Stefano frowned. "Fallon?"

Yes, it was Fallon. He could hear the tap of her heels coming up the stairs. Quickly, he ran his hands through his damp hair. She was early. He hadn't had time to make the Margaritas or chill two glasses...

"Stefano."

He swung toward the bedroom door. He'd only been gone a few hours but seeing her reminded him of how he'd missed her.

"Cara..."

Whoa. That look on her face. Cold eyes, rigid posture. Trouble was coming, with a capital *T*.

"What's wrong?"

Fallon tossed her purse in the direction of the dresser. It landed on the carpet instead, but she made no move to pick it up. Neither, after another look at her eyes, did Stefano.

"Wrong? Why should anything be wrong?"

"Well, I don't know. You look—you look—"

"What? Angry? Furious?" She crossed her arms and glared at him. "How do I look, Stefano?"

"Upset," he said warily.

"Good guess."

"Sweetheart." He cleared his throat. Something had gone wrong. *Carla,* he thought instantly, and started toward Fallon. "Does this have anything to do with—with what we talked about last night?"

"As I recall, we didn't talk about anything last night. Correction. I talked. You danced."

He paused a couple of feet away. "Danced?" he said, even more warily. "I don't understand."

"Oh, it's simple. I talked. I asked questions. You danced around them. Why should I quit my job? Why shouldn't I work for Carla? Because you wanted it that way, that was why."

Fallon could feel her pulse racing. All the way here, she'd imagined what she'd say to Stefano. She hadn't really sorted out the words but she'd reached one sure conclusion.

She wouldn't cry. Wouldn't tell him how humiliating it had been, learning about him and Carla the way she had. Wouldn't tell him that it killed her, *killed* her, to know he'd made love to Carla in that same bed in the *castello* where he'd made love to her, in the same bed here in his apartment, that Carla had walked out on him and her leaving had angered him so much that he'd become vengeful and taken another woman on the rebound.

"You son of a bitch," she said, and all her good intentions flew out the window. "Why didn't you tell me you'd been Carla's lover?"

"*Cara*. Sweetheart—"

"Do not 'cara' me. Do not 'sweetheart' me! Do you know what it was like, hearing about your affair from her?" Fallon rushed forward and slammed her hands against Stefano's chest. "How would you like it if you were at a meeting and the man you were doing business with leaned over, smirked and said, 'I used to sleep with Fallon O'Connell.'"

"I'd kill him," Stefano said darkly.

"Ha!"

She hit him again and Stefano caught her wrists.

"Listen," he said, "I know I should have told you."

"She walked out on you. That was why you wouldn't let us into that—that crypt you call a castle, why you spied on us while we worked. She walked out and you were miserably unhappy."

"I threw her out."

"So you claim."

"I threw her out, Fallon. I wouldn't let any of your crew into the *castello* because I'd never wanted to let Carla use it in the first place."

"Oh, please. As long as she was sleeping with you, you were happy to give her whatever she wanted, but when she broke up with you—"

Stefano's expression turned grim. "Is that what she says? It's a lie."

She wanted to believe him, oh, she wanted to, but he'd lied to her already. Why wouldn't he lie again?

"As for why I watched you work, I told you the reason." His hands tightened on her wrists. "I was watching *you*. Only you. That day at the airport changed everything. I saw you, I wanted you—"

"And you always get what you want. Isn't that how you view life?"

Stefano let go of her, spun on his heel and strode across the room. He muttered something his Sicilian grandmother would have erased with a mouthful of soap, then stalked toward Fallon again.

"I'm not going to fight with you," he said as calmly as he could. "I admit, I should have told you."

"Yes. You should have. If you lo— If you respected me, you'd have at least told me last night."

"You're right. I did a stupid thing." He hesitated. He had news that would make her happy, but how could he tell it to her when she was almost shaking with anger?

"Fallon."

"If you're going to try and sweet-talk your way out of this—"

"I'm not." He reached for her. She let him cup her shoulders but she wouldn't let him draw her to him. All right. He deserved what she was doing to him but that would all change in a minute. "Don't you want to know where I was today?"

"No."

So much for the easy lead-in. "I flew to Boston, to see an old friend."

"How nice for you. Did you sleep with her, too?"

"For God's sake, Fallon!" Stefano let go of her, took a steadying breath. "I'm trying to tell you something important. Something I know will make you happy."

That you love me, Fallon thought, so clearly, so distinctly, that for an instant she was afraid she'd spoken aloud. Because that was the only thing she wanted to hear, the only thing that could make what had happened today fade away.

That was what her anger was about, what everything was about. She needed to hear Stefano say, *I love you. I love you exactly as you are. I've never loved anyone else, never wanted anyone else, as I love you.*

"Sweetheart."

Her eyes met his. Something glittered in those deep brown depths, something she'd never seen there before. Her heart lurched. She felt as if she were going to do something really stupid, like faint or throw herself into his arms and say, *I know what you're going to tell me, Stefano, and I love you, too.*

"I have something for you," he said softly.

He reached into his pocket. Fallon's heart did an unsteady two-step. All her life, she'd thought stuff like marriage proposals and engagement rings were for other women. Now, she knew they were the most important things in the world, and what else could Stefano be taking from his pocket but a ring? What else would make him hold out his hand as if he were handing her the earth?

A piece of paper. That's what. A paper with a couple of names and phone numbers scrawled on it.

She took it, stared at it, then at him.

"I don't understand. What is this?"

He smiled, as if he were giving her not just the earth but the sun and the moon, too.

"The names of the two best plastic surgeons in New York. If anybody can make you look the way you once did, it's one of them."

He was smiling. He looked so happy. So smug. So certain he was handing her something that would solve all their problems.

"The way I once did?" she said in a papery whisper. "Like Fallon O'Connell, supermodel. Is that what you mean, Stefano?"

He nodded. She nodded, too. Then she tore the paper in half, dropped it at his feet as she walked out of the bedroom.

He called her name, shouted at her to come back, ran after her and reached for her, but she shrugged him off and kept on walking, out of his apartment and out of his life.

CHAPTER TWELVE

FALLON stepped from the elevator and almost ran through the lobby of Stefano's apartment building.

The doorman smiled and touched a finger to his hat.

"Afternoon, Miss O'Connell. Do you want a—"

"No," Fallon said, and brushed past him.

Of course she wanted a taxi. She wanted a rocket to Mars, whatever would get her out of here fast, but if the doorman hailed a cab for her he'd be able to tell Stefano where she was going...

And she never wanted to see him again.

Never.

He'd ripped out her heart.

He'd let her traipse into Carla's office like a lamb going to slaughter and followed it up by making it crystal clear he was tired of playing the martyr. He wanted her to turn into Fallon O'Connell again, *the* Fallon O'Connell, and just in case the message wasn't clear enough, he'd gotten her the names of not one but two surgeons.

He'd probably expected her to throw herself into his arms with gratitude.

The stupid, insensitive, heartless son of a bitch!

All that nonsense about wanting her for herself, about seeing who she really was...

She reached the corner as the light turned red. Traffic ground through the clogged intersection; caught in the knot of impatient pedestrians on the sidewalk, Fallon choked back an angry sob.

She knew who she was. She was a woman with a

scarred face and a liar for a lover, and the sooner she took back control of her life—

"Fallon? Fallon!"

Fallon craned her neck and looked back. Stefano was running toward her. He looked upset and angry.

Angry? What did *he* have to be angry about?

The light was still red, cars were moving bumper to bumper, but she darted off the curb and dodged through them. Horns blared, drivers cursed.

Fallon didn't care.

All she wanted was to get away.

"Fallon," Stefano shouted, "damn it, stop! Have you gone crazy?"

Maybe she *had* been crazy. Now, she was sane. She didn't want to see him, hear his lies, look into his eyes and know what a fool she'd been to have fallen in love with him.

Another intersection. Another red light—and an empty taxi, idling at the head of a long line of vehicles. Fallon dashed for the cab, pulled the door open and hurled herself inside.

"Drive," she gasped.

The cabbie shot her a look in the mirror. "Where to?"

"Anywhere. Just get moving."

She looked back. Stefano was halfway to the corner. He was panting, running hard, still shouting her name. People were staring at him, even blasé New Yorkers who'd long ago learned that the secret to survival was not to see anything you didn't want to see.

"Just go," she said urgently.

The light changed. The cabbie glanced in the mirror again.

"I don' wan' no trouble, miss."

"No trouble. See that man? He's—he's my husband. I found him with another woman. I'll give you an extra twenty if he doesn't catch us."

Stefano was almost at the cab. His face was red. "Fallon!" he yelled.

"Fifty dollars," she said desperately. "Fifty dollars to get me out of here."

The cabbie nodded, stepped on the gas and left Fifth Avenue and Stefano Lucchesi far behind.

Two blocks later, Fallon told the driver to take her to La Guardia airport.

Going to her apartment was out of the question. That was surely the first place Stefano would check. The airport was safer.

She was lucky. A flight to Vegas was about to board and yes, there was a seat left.

An hour into the flight, Fallon made three phone calls. One to her agent, one to Carla's office at *Bridal Dreams,* one to the concierge at her apartment building in Soho.

"Jackie?" she said, when her agent answered, "it's Fallon. In case you need me, I'll be in London for a week or so."

"Why would I need you?" Jackie asked in bewilderment, but Fallon had already broken the connection.

Next, she called Carla's office.

"In case Carla didn't mention it," Fallon told her secretary, "I quit."

The girl laughed. "So does anybody with half a brain. You want to pick up your check or should I mail it?"

"Actually, I'll be in San Francisco for a couple of weeks. I'll pick it up when I get back."

Setting up the final diversion was the simplest.

"Jason," she told the concierge in the building where she owned a condo, "it's Fallon O'Connell. I know, I know. Well, I've been—I've been away. And I'm going away again. Tokyo. Right. So if anyone should come looking for me... Thanks. That should do just fine."

She hung up the phone. The west coast, the Far East and the United Kingdom. Stefano would keep his minions busy for a while. By the time he figured out she really had no wish to see him again, his interest in finding her would have vanished.

The man was in the middle of a losing streak. Neither of his last two women had lasted very long, and both had walked out on him.

That, at least, was some satisfaction. But the truth was, sooner or later, he wouldn't even remember her.

Never mind.

Right now, she had to think about what she'd say to her mother when she reached Vegas.

Hi, Ma, here I am and oh, yes, my face is a mess, isn't it?

Hi, Ma, it's me and why would you think something was wrong just because I've turned up on your doorstep without so much as a toothbrush?

Fallon closed her eyes and leaned her head back. She'd offer a simple story. No details, no dramatics and above all, no tears.

Not one.

She thought it was an excellent plan until her mother opened the door to the O'Connell penthouse at the Desert Song Hotel and Casino, took one look at her and said, "Oh, Fallon. Oh, my darling girl…"

"Oh, Ma," Fallon sobbed, and flung herself into her mother's waiting arms.

A week later, Mary Elizabeth O'Connell Coyle and her husband, Dan, stood close together in their bedroom, whispering like children plotting.

"I don't know what to do with her," Mary said. "She's always been so logical, so focused. Now she stays in the guest room and hardly comes out."

"Well, the accident…"

"No, it's not that. What happened must have devastated her—God knows, it did me—but I can tell that she's come to grips with the scars. It's something else, an ache inside her that goes deeper than the wounds left by the accident.''

"I don't understand."

"She mentioned a man's name when she came here last week. She said he was a particularly persistent reporter and if he phoned, I was to say I had no idea where she was.''

"Well, that makes sense. Those vermin would sell their own mothers for a buck.''

"No, this is different. She got this sad look when she mentioned him. He's no reporter, Daniel. Fallon wants to avoid him, but I'm sure it's for more personal reasons.''

"You think he hurt her?" Dan narrowed his eyes. He had his own grown children but Mary's were almost as dear to him. "Tell me his name. I'll find the bastard and teach him what it means to hurt a girl of ours.''

Mary smiled. Who'd ever have imagined, at this stage in her life, she'd find another wonderful man to love?

"I know you would," she said gently, "but I really don't think that's the solution for this kind of hurt.''

"Well then, what is?"

"I don't know." Mary sighed. "Fallon's always been so independent. Even when she was little. 'What's the matter?' I'd say, if I found her looking upset, and she'd say, 'Nothing's the matter, Mother,' in a tone that made it clear she wanted me to mind my own business.''

"Stubborn."

"Very."

Dan grinned. "I can't imagine where she'd get such a trait, Duchess. Can you?"

Mary laughed softly. Almost everyone who knew her referred to her as the duchess but few said it to her face. Her sons did, and now Daniel, and she loved the term of affection on his lips.

"I know. She's like me, more so than any of my daughters. But I feel useless.''

"Fallon's tough. She's got your genes. All she needs is a little time."

"Ah, but time slips away so easily. You and I have lived long enough to know that."

Dan sighed and drew his wife close. "Well, I don't know what other options you have, dear. She's a grown woman."

"You're right." Mary patted Dan's chest, then stepped back. "Go on. I know you have a security meeting scheduled."

"Will you be all right?"

"I'll be fine. Fallon and I will have coffee, and I'll see if I can get her to talk to me."

"And if she won't?"

"Then I'll talk to her. See if I can get her Irish up. A little anger would be better than moping."

Dan chuckled.

"What?" Mary said.

"Felonious mopery. That's what we used to call it when I was on the job in New York, if you saw some guy just hanging around the streets, doing nothing. Felonious mopery."

"Police talk for what ails my daughter," Mary said, and laughed. They smiled at each other. Then she smoothed down the collar of her husband's shirt. "I have to do something about it, of course."

"Of course. But what?"

Mary shrugged her shoulders. "Something," she said in a quiet voice.

"Mary. Look at me."

Daniel put his hand under his wife's chin and lifted her face to his.

"Go on," she said gently. "Go to that meeting. I'll see you later."

"Why do I get the feeling I ought to stay right here?"

"Because you still have the instincts of a policeman.

And those same instincts should tell you there are times it's better to know as little as possible about a situation.''

Daniel gave a deep sigh. "I'll be in my office downstairs, Duchess, if you need me.''

Mary smiled. "I'll remember that.''

She walked him to the front door and gave a sidelong glance to the guest room on her way back. The door was shut. It was always shut. After that one outburst when she'd arrived, Fallon hadn't said more than a dozen words; she stayed in her room except for meals, when she came to the table and poked at her food.

It was the housekeeper's afternoon off. Rather than call down for room service, Mary went into the kitchen, made fresh coffee and filled a serving tray with all the necessities for a civilized coffee break. At the guest-room door, she hesitated, then cleared her throat.

"Fallon?''

"Yes?''

"I've brought us some coffee.''

"Thank you, but I don't want any.''

"Jenny made some of those oatmeal scones you always loved.''

"I'll have one later.''

Time to play a mother's ace card, Mary thought, and sighed.

"I'm supposed to take an afternoon break, Fallon. The doctor says so, and I've gotten in the habit of coffee—decaf, of course—at about this hour, but if you don't want to join me—''

The door opened, as she'd known it would.

"Thank you, darling,'' Mary said, brushing past her daughter, determinedly ignoring the lifeless expression and drooping body language even though those things troubled her more than the scars. They spoke of a deeper wound that might be harder to heal.

"Would you like to go out on the terrace, Fallon? It's

hot, but it's a lovely clear day and the air will do us both good.''

''First tell me why the doctor wants you to take a break in the afternoon. You said your last tests were fine.''

''And they are.'' Mary nodded at the sliding doors. ''Would you, darling? Thank you.'' The women stepped outside, both of them blinking in the sudden glare of the sun.

''If your tests were fine, why did he tell you to take a break?''

''Well, he did say that when I first got out of the hospital, but my heart's sound now.'' Mary put the tray on a round glass-topped table. ''I just stretched the facts, that's all. How else was I going to get you to open your door?''

''Letting me think there was something wrong with you wasn't very nice, Mother.''

''No,'' Mary said blithely, ''it wasn't. It's awful when someone you love lets you worry needlessly, isn't it?''

''That's sneaky, Ma. And it's not the same thing at all. I'm not making you worry about me. You're doing it all on your own. I told you what happened. I drove into a tree and cut my face.''

''That's not what's brought you here,'' Mary said as she filled their cups. ''I know you like cream in your coffee but I'm never sure if you're dieting or not.''

''No need to diet,'' Fallon said with forced gaiety, ''now that I'm not modeling anymore.''

''But your figure will still matter to you.''

''I suppose. Is that what you want to talk about? My figure? My future? What I'm going to do with myself, now that I'm finished modeling?''

''Are you?'' Mary said bluntly. ''Finished modeling? What about makeup? Or surgery?''

Fallon's face turned white. ''Don't tell me. You want to recommend a surgeon, too.''

''No, I don't have any... Too?''

''Forget it, Mother.''

"I only meant—"

"I know what you meant. You'd like to see me look like my old self again."

"I'd like to see you with some spirit again," Mary said, "and if all this moping is because of the scarring on your face, then I think you might want to consider doing something about it."

"I'm not moping."

"On the other hand," Mary went on, as if Fallon hadn't spoken, "the scars don't detract in the least from your looks."

"Ha!"

"Besides, I seem to recall that the last time we saw each other, you said something about being tired of the business and wanting a change."

"I did. I just didn't expect the decision to be taken out of my hands."

"Life's like that sometimes. Things happen, choices are made whether you want them or not." Mary held out the platter of scones. "Want one?"

"No, thank you."

The women sipped their coffee in silence. Then Mary put down her cup.

"The man you mentioned, the reporter—"

"What about him?"

"He has an Italian name. Did you meet him in Sicily?"

"You know, Ma, you have this infuriating habit of asking questions but not answering them."

"Do I?"

A smile flickered on Fallon's lips, then faded. "Yes."

"This Steven Lucchesi—"

"Stefano Lucchesi."

"Right. What magazine does he write for?"

Fallon hesitated. Had she said Stefano wrote for a magazine? The day she'd arrived was a blur. She remembered seeing Mary's face, seeing her open arms, knowing she had to protect herself from Stefano, should he somehow track her here...

"Fallon? Who does he write for?"

"He's—he's freelance."

"I see. Did you meet in Sicily?"

"Why would you think that?"

"Well, the Italian name..."

"He's an American. And yes, we met in Sicily." What did a few details matter? Her mood was rotten, her temper mean, and her mother wasn't going to leave her alone until she'd pried some answers out of her.

"Was he on assignment to get photos of you?"

"No. Not exactly."

"But he got some."

"Mother..."

"And he's driven you crazy since then."

Fallon's eyes flashed. Wonderful, Mary thought. It was her daughter's first real reaction to anything since that outburst of emotion when she'd arrived.

"Why are you asking all these questions, Ma? Has Stefano called?"

"Stefano?" Mary raised her eyebrows. "Interesting, that you're on a first name basis with a reporter you despise."

"Just remember, if he calls—"

"I don't know where you are."

"Exactly."

"Because he's a persistent reporter."

"Right."

"And not just a man who's trying to find a woman who ran away from him."

"Absolutely ri—" Fallon blinked. "What?"

"Dan thinks your Mr. Lucchesi mistreated you," Mary said casually. "But I said, a woman doesn't mope around the house—"

"Who said anything about running away? And I have not moped!"

"And cry in her sleep—"

"I most certainly do not cry in my—"

"Yes, you do. And a woman doesn't do those things over a man who's been cruel to her. Not a woman with O'Connell blood in her veins."

Fallon shot to her feet. "What on earth are you talking about?"

Mary looked at her daughter. "I don't know," she said calmly. "Not in any detail. I only know what I think, which is that you and this Mr. Lucchesi had a lovers' quarrel—"

"A lovers' quarrel?" Fallon slapped her hands on her hips. There was fire in her eyes and her chin was high. Mary wanted to grab her and hug her and welcome her back...but she knew better.

"Yes," she said, still calmly, "a lovers' spat, and you left him and now you regret it, and—"

"I do not regret a thing! Stefano Lucchesi is a self-centered, self-indulgent son of a bitch!" Fallon strode to the end of the terrace, turned sharply and strode back. "I never want to see him again."

"Because?"

"Because he's a liar and a cheat. Because he used me. Because—because—"

"Because you fell in love with him, and he fell in love with you, and neither one of you was smart enough to know when it was time to admit it."

Fallon felt her heart stand still. That wasn't her mother's voice. It wasn't Dan's. It was—it was—

She swung around. Stefano stood in the open door to the terrace, his hands on his hips, just as hers were; his eyes shooting sparks, just as hers were.

He looked awful. Disheveled, as if he'd been sleeping in his custom-made suit. As if he'd run his hands through his dark hair a hundred times. As if the stubble on his face hadn't seen a razor in a week...

And she, oh God, she loved him!

A whole week of telling herself she'd never loved him, that she'd confused gratitude with love, went sailing into the blue Las Vegas sky. A whole week of chastising herself for ever having returned to the States with him, turned into nonsense.

She loved him, this man who'd hurt her, she loved him...

And what was that he'd said? That he loved her?

"Yes," he said grimly, his eyes locked to hers so that she knew she'd spoken the words aloud, "I love you, though I'm damned if I know why I should. To walk out on me, just when I was about to tell you what you mean to me. To run from me and leave me with half a dozen blind alleys to search—"

"Three," Fallon said, her voice trembling.

"Tokyo. London. San Francisco." His eyes narrowed; he came toward her slowly, one step at a time. Dimly, Fallon saw her mother stand up, smile at her, touch Stefano's shoulder and slide the terrace door closed behind her. "Do you have any idea what a week in hell is?" Stefano grabbed her shoulders. "I sloshed around London in the rain for two days, drove the streets in San Francisco until I never wanted to see one again, got to Japan just in time for a damned typhoon—"

"A couple of lessons in humility never hurt anybody."

"Is that what this was all about? Did you think I needed to be humbled?" His hands tightened on her. "I love you. Didn't that mean anything to you?"

"You don't love me," she said, and tried to pull free. He wouldn't let her. Instead, he jerked her to her toes.

"Don't tell me what I do or don't do, damn it! Your mother's the same piece of work you are. I phoned, I said I was crazy in love with you and if she knew where you were, she had to tell me, and she said, 'you don't love my daughter or you wouldn't have broken her heart.'" His voice roughened. "And I said, Mrs. O'Connell—"

"Coyle," Fallon said numbly, while her brain tried to process what was happening. "My mother's name is—"

"I said, Mrs. O'Connell, I didn't break your daughter's heart, she broke mine. There I was, about to do something I'd sworn I'd never do, get down on one knee and say, 'Fallon, I love you. I adore you. I need you more than I need breath. Will you marry me?' and instead of giving me the chance to say all that, your daughter tore my heart in pieces and dropped it on the floor."

"I tore up a slip of paper," Fallon said, her voice trembling, "because you wanted Fallon O'Connell, supermodel, instead of the Fallon O'Connell who lives inside me."

"That's crap!"

"You want me to have surgery on my face."

"I want you to smile again, damn it."

"That's it. Make it sound as if the surgery was for me, not for—"

Stefano kissed her to silence. His mouth was hard against hers and why wouldn't it be? he thought furiously. He wanted to shake her, to turn her over his knee, to make her know that he'd almost lost his mind when he'd thought he'd lost her.

Maybe he had. She wasn't kissing him back, wasn't doing anything...

And then, slowly, her lips softened against his. Her hands rose and clutched his shirt. She made a soft, sweet little sound that he'd been afraid he'd never hear her make again.

His kiss gentled and he gathered her in his arms. At last, he took his mouth from hers.

"I love you," he said gruffly. "Can you imagine what it did to me when I saw the shadows in your eyes? I realized you were hurting inside, that I was being selfish, that if it weren't for me you'd have contacted a surgeon—and then you confirmed it all, the night before you ran away."

"Confirmed what?" Fallon said in confusion.

"Don't you remember? You asked me how I'd feel, if you had surgery." He cupped her face in his hands. "That was when I knew it was time to stop lying to myself and pretending that my love for you was enough to heal you. You have to do what's right for you, not for me."

"Oh, Stefano. All this time, I thought…" She touched his cheek. "But the names of those doctors—"

"The friend in Boston I told you about is a doctor. He gave me their names. If you want surgery, then I want you to have the best. And I'll be with you, every step of the way."

Fallon gave a watery little laugh. "*You* want the surgery because you think *I* want it?"

"I told you, I've been selfish—"

"You?" She shook her head and wound her arms around his neck. "You're the most generous man in the world, Stefano. I thought you wanted me to have surgery. That you couldn't look at me without pitying me, and I don't want pity from you, I want—"

"What, sweetheart? What do you want? My heart? My soul? My life? They're all yours. I wanted to wait and tell you these things when you were whole. I was afraid if I rushed things, I'd take advantage of you."

Fallon laughed. She rose on her toes and pressed her mouth to his.

"I love you," she said. "I've always loved you, don't you know that?"

Stefano kissed her again and again, until she was clinging to him. Then he leaned his forehead against hers.

"I should have told you about Carla," he said in a low voice. "But I couldn't figure out a way to tell the woman I loved that I'd slept with a woman she knew, much less the woman she was working for. Not when things suddenly seemed precarious. You'd stopped smiling, stopped looking at me with something special glowing in your eyes."

Fallon nodded. He'd made mistakes, but so had she.

All that mattered was that they loved each other and that they'd found each other again.

"Fallon. Sweetheart, will you be my wife?"

She smiled. The look on Stefano's face was one she'd thought she'd never see again.

"Yes," she said softly. "Oh, yes, my love, I will."

He drew her close and kissed her.

On the other side of the glass doors, Mary Elizabeth O'Connell Coyle put her hand to her lips. Eyes damp, she drew the blinds, picked up the phone and dialed Special Guest Services.

"This is Mary O'Connell Coyle," she said. "Susan, you know that lovely wedding you did for Daniel and me? What if I wanted to plan one that was just a little bit bigger..."

EPILOGUE

MEGAN O'CONNELL gazed at herself in the mirrored wall of the guest suite bedroom at *Castello Lucchesi*, stroked a hand down the long skirt of her pale yellow maid-of-honor gown, and sighed.

"Lovely," she said in a dreamy voice.

Briana, standing beside her in an identical gown, smoothed back an auburn curl and looked at her sister's reflection.

"Such modesty," she said sweetly.

"I was talking about the gown."

"Oh," Bree said.

The sisters' eyes met. Meg stuck out her tongue. Bree grinned and stuck hers out, too.

"In that case, I'll have to agree. The gowns are gorgeous."

"And what a cool idea Fallon had," Meg said, "asking us both to be her maid of honor."

"And me to be her bridesmaid," Cassie Bercovic O'Connell said. She stepped toward the mirror. "Especially now."

All three women dropped their gaze to Cassie's round belly. Their eyes met in the glass and they started to giggle.

"I look like an elephant," Cassie said.

"Hey."

The women turned. Keir, Sean and Cullen stood in the open doorway, tall and handsome in black tuxes.

"I resent that." Keir smiled at his wife. "You look," he said softly, "like an incredibly beautiful woman."

Cassie laughed as she went to him. "An incredibly pregnant, incredibly beautiful woman, you mean."

"You're all beautiful," Cullen said gallantly, which earned him a round of female applause.

"He's right," Meg said, "we are. Us in pale yellow, Cassie in pale green, Ma downstairs in sapphire—"

"And Fallon in to-die-for white satin." Bree sighed dramatically. "She almost makes being a bride seem like a good idea."

Megan shuddered. "Bite your tongue!"

"Well, of course I didn't mean it was a good idea for you or me. It's just that Fallon's so happy. Oh, and you, too, Cassie... Damn. I'm putting both feet in my mouth, aren't I?"

"Yeah," Cullen said amiably, "but you usually do."

"Go on, ruin that nice stuff you said a couple of minutes ago."

"Well, you paid me to say—*oof!* Hell, Bree. Elbows like that would be considered lethal weapons in some states."

"I'm just glad you didn't see what an awful bunch of men you were getting as brothers-in-law before you told Keir you'd marry him," Meg told Cassie. "Or we might have lost you before we got you!"

"Yes," Cassie said with affection, "they're reprobates of the first order."

"And now we'll have another male on the O'Connell team," Sean said. "Well, he's a Lucchesi, but you know what I mean."

"He's a good guy," Keir said. "He's crazy about Fallon."

"And he knows how to win a battle without spilling blood," Cullen added. "I mean, I'm sure Ma had her heart set on making this wedding at the Desert Song."

"She did. But your sister and I explained that the *castello* means everything to us."

The O'Connell clan turned as one. Stefano stood in the doorway, wearing a tux, looking as serious and as nervous as they all figured a man was supposed to be on his wedding day.

"I just want to tell you... I love Fallon with all my heart. I know how you cherish her and I promise you, I'll cherish her, too."

There was a moment of silence. Then Stefano's soon-to-be sisters-in-law sniffed and reached for the lace hankies they'd conveniently tucked into their gowns. His new brothers-in-law cleared their throats. And Mary Elizabeth, looking as regal as a duchess, beamed at her growing family as she sailed into the room.

"For the record, once I saw this magnificent castle, I wanted the wedding here, too." Mary looked at Stefano. "It's time," she said softly.

"Yes," he said, and the smile that lit his face made the women weep all over again.

Fallon and her bridegroom took their vows on the terrace, beneath a bower woven from a dazzling array of flowers.

It was better to stick with one or two varieties, the wedding planner had told them, but Stefano and Fallon smiled and said they wanted roses and tulips, orchids and hyacinths, violets and pansies and wildflowers.

The breeze was gentle and warm, scented by the sea and the flowers as it whispered over the assembled guests.

Stefano held Fallon's hand throughout the ceremony. His eyes never left his bride's face. Her scars were still there, but they were invisible to her, to him, to anyone who knew her.

They'd written the vows themselves, so the words had special meaning. And, though nobody knew it, they'd already planned another ceremony only for the family at the

Desert Song. But this ceremony, this place, would always be their very own.

The last words of the ancient ritual that binds man and woman through all eternity sighed away on the breeze.

"Stefano," the justice said, "you may kiss your bride."

Stefano smiled and gathered his wife into his arms. *"Cara,"* he whispered, *"Ti amo."*

Fallon smiled, too. *"Mo ghrá,"* she whispered back, *"gráim thú."*

Sean shifted closer to Cullen. "What in heck was that?"

Cullen cleared his throat. "Fine Irishman you are, bro. It was Gaelic. She called him her heart and said she loved him."

"Wow." Sean smiled. "Serious stuff."

"Very."

Cullen watched his sister kiss her new husband. He looked at his mother and his stepfather, holding hands like a pair of kids. His dark blue gaze moved to Keir, who stood with his arm around Cassie. Keir's hand was on his wife's hip but his fingers were splayed possessively over her rounded belly.

Cullen's throat tightened. The world seemed to tilt. He remembered a woman. A night. A memory that was little more than a whisper in the matrix of time.

"Cullen?" Sean leaned in. "You okay?"

"Sure." Cullen cleared his throat. "Warm out here, that's all."

"What you need is a glass of champagne."

The string quartet began playing the recessional. Stefano and Fallon turned toward their guests, who rose to their feet, smiling and applauding. The O'Connell brothers shook hands, kissed the women in their family and Sean, always ready for a party, reached behind a flower arrangement and held a magnum of Cristal aloft.

"Ta-da!"

The O'Connells cheered. Sean popped the cork, Keir produced glasses, and the pale golden wine began to flow.

"This'll cure whatever ails you," he told Cullen.

"Sounds like a plan," Cullen replied, and the world turned right side up again.

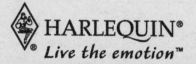

The world's bestselling romance series.

HARLEQUIN®
Presents

Seduction and Passion Guaranteed!

Your dream ticket to the vacation of a lifetime!

Why not relax and allow Harlequin Presents® to whisk you away
to stunning international locations with our new miniseries...

FOREIGN AFFAIRS

Where irresistible men and sophisticated women
surrender to seduction under the golden sun.

Don't miss this opportunity to
experience glamorous lifestyles
and exotic settings in:

**Robyn Donald's
THE TEMPTRESS OF TARIKA BAY
on sale July, #2336**

**THE FRENCH COUNT'S MISTRESS
by Susan Stephens
on sale August, #2342**

**THE SPANIARD'S WOMAN
by Diana Hamilton
on sale September, #2346**

**THE ITALIAN MARRIAGE
by Kathryn Ross
on sale October, #2353**

FOREIGN AFFAIRS... A world full of passion!

**Pick up a Harlequin Presents® novel and you will enter a world
of spine-tingling passion and provocative, tantalizing romance!**

Available wherever Harlequin books are sold.

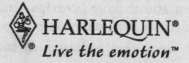

HARLEQUIN®
Live the emotion™

Visit us at www.eHarlequin.com

HPFAMA